CONGRESSIONAL PROCLIVITIES

The Gender-Flipped Version

Parliamentary Desires Book 2

HG Jones

Michelle Morgan is a busy contractor with a skill for negotiating major deals where all others fail. Following her successful negotiation of a global trade deal, she and her new ally, Charlotte Adams have been given a new task together. American President Geoffrey Nash has requested their assistance and expertise in negotiating important gun law reforms through the Congress.

It's a task that will take Michelle all the negotiation skills she has, taking her across the United States. Her adventure will introduce her to a range of larger-than-life characters, from the curious Gregory Miller, to Floridian alligator farmer, Roberta "Gator" Hill. But things are not all that they seem, and Michelle will need to develop some new skills, and quickly.

Follow Michelle and Charlotte as they negotiate the biggest gun law reform in American history, using their best tools for the job – their pussies.

Contents

CHAPTER 1 – Mile High

Day: Tuesday
Time: 1600 hours
Location: Canberra, Australia

Michelle Morgan stopped and checked her watch. It was the only moment she'd had to herself all day, her one brief second of peace amongst the noise of the world. There were only a few hours remaining before she was expected at the airport.

Looking around her humble apartment, nestled within the leafy heart of Canberra, she mentally ran through the list of items she needed to pack. She wished she'd been given more to prepare, but sometimes offers arise that you cannot refuse, even if they are somewhat inconvenient.

She recalled the glint in Charlotte Adams' eye when she'd asked her on the lawn at Government House to work with her on a top-secret mission in Washington, DC. Despite only meeting a few days prior, Michelle still wasn't sure whether the beautiful woman from the Deep South was her lover, her sidekick, or her negotiations partner – or if she was all three.

Once her adversary, after working together to secure the Trans-Global Trade Partnership, the relationship was hard to define. All Michelle knew was that Charlotte Adams was a woman who knew how to fuck. But now, Michelle was heading into new territory. She was going to be on Charlotte's turf, on her home soil, working her ass to the bone for her.

Of course, it had only taken her a matter of seconds before she agreed to the request. After all, she was only human, and there was nothing more human in Michelle's eyes than going to town on a Southern gentlewoman like Charlotte Adams. Even as she daydreamed and fantasised to herself, she could feel her vagina starting to moisten in her racy red G-string.

"Not now," she muttered to herself. There'd be plenty of time for that later, and hopefully plenty of times. She'd never met anybody like Charlotte before. She was quick as a whip, smart and intuitive, which made her an excellent negotiator, but also a phenomenal lover.

By the time she had finished packing, there were three suitcases, all filled to maximum capacity. The first two contained all the clothing she required for an extended period of time, everything from dresses and skirts to intimates. In her line of business, Michelle didn't have the pleasure of forward planning, and required an outfit for every occasion. Although Charlotte said this deal that she was working on would only take a few days to finalise, there was no way of knowing exactly how long she would be staying Stateside. Days could become weeks, and weeks months. What mattered most to Michelle was that they get the job done, and done properly.

The third suitcase was where she'd packed all the business essentials: vibrators, dildos, butt plugs, flesh toys, clitoral stimulants, whips and chains, nipple clamps, gloves, lubricants, her laptop, among other necessities. It was essential for Michelle to be prepared wherever she went. You never knew when you'd need a vibrating butt plug, and she certainly didn't want to be caught lacking.

The negotiations business could be a fickle beast at times. It was more than simply 'you suck my clit, and I'll suck yours'; it was much closer to stroking a G-spot with only one finger, and required all her mental attention, her finesse and tenderness, and a whole lot of lubrication. There was an art to bringing a man or woman to the brink of the most powerful orgasm they'd ever experienced, then, like a viper, striking at them with her list of demands.

She was so invested in selecting the perfect dildos from her vast collection, that Michelle barely noticed her phone was ringing. It was only after the caller's second attempt that she registered the sound of shiny glass vibrating against the wood of her bedside table. "Hello," she answered politely.

"It's me," said Charlotte in her usual Americana drawl. "The airport transfer is on the way here now. I'm going to be outside yours in ten minutes."

"Fuck," Michelle swore as she hung up the phone. Only ten minutes! She wasn't ready yet, not while she was still deciding between the purple vibrating dildo, and the black dildo with realistic veins and ridges down the shaft. In a moment of panic and anticipation, she threw them both into the suitcase. If she was over the baggage limit, she would instruct the airline to bill the Australian Government instead. After everything they'd put her through, it was the least they owed her.

Time flew by, and before she knew it, Charlotte's taxi was outside, beeping its horn noisily. With great effort, Michelle lugged her bags and suitcases down the stairs to the street level.

"Hey, babe," said Charlotte, leaning casually against the passenger door. She leaned over and kissed Michelle full on the mouth.

Michelle blushed for the first time since her late teens. Charlotte had never called her 'babe' before. What did that mean? Did she see them as some sort of couple? Was Michelle even ready for a relationship, even if it was with the woman who had given her the most intense orgasms of her life? She decided to put it out of her head. It was probably just a Southern belle tradition to call someone 'babe'.

Once her suitcases were loaded in to the boot of the taxi, they were on their way to the airport. Michelle was sat in the rear, while Charlotte up front. She couldn't help but ponder about Charlotte's words to her. *Babe.* Michelle had only been in love once before, a long time ago now, but there was something that sparked in er heart that made her feel like she could learn to feel that way about another person again one day. She might even be able to feel that for Charlotte.

She remained silent on the trip to the airport, which fortunately only took a few minutes. *At least*, she thought to herself, *it isn't uncomfortable silence*. She was, however, relieved when the taxi pulled up at the airport. They weren't using the main terminal today, but were using the special access area designated for international diplomats and politicians.

"I represent the President when I'm travelling to Australia," explained Charlotte, "so I get treated like him when I'm in town. Wait until you see what we're flying home in."

Michelle didn't have to wait long until she saw a private jet, emblazoned with the US President's seal, along with an enormous American flag design that covered the exterior of the fuselage. "Are you trying to impress me?" she asked playfully.

"Yeah, maybe a little bit," replied Charlotte with a grin.

Michelle had an unfamiliar pang in her stomach. Was Charlotte leading her on? Or was she was just reading too much into the situation? Surely, she wouldn't be able to manage a relationship with Charlotte, especially given the line of work they were in. No, it was definitely time she gets her act together and stop thinking like a love-sick teen. She would fuck Charlotte, for business and maybe pleasure, but that would be the limit to their association. She had made her mind up, and that was final.

"Come on," said Charlotte, "it's time to board."

Sure enough, the staff had already taken their bags, treating them as treasures from the unknown deep as they gently carried the across the tarmac and loaded them into the hull of the plane. When the time came, official guards came and collected the two women, pausing briefly to roll out a red carpet, before allowing them to walk together. As Charlotte reached the top of the stairs, she turned, and saluted the ground staff, who saluted to her in return. Michelle paid them the same respect, before stepping aboard the aircraft.

She'd only flown in a private jet once before, though had been on board the Prime Minister's personal plane, an aircraft he'd affectionately dubbed the *Hawaiian Express*. Michelle didn't understand the reference, but presumed it had something to do with drugs.

"You should take your seat quickly," said an air hostess, a shorter, older woman, with very short cut hair and lots of tattoos on her exposed arms. The words 'bull dyke' popped into Michelle's head when she looked at her properly. She looked like she could be part of one of those alt-right fan clubs she'd seen pop up on the news from time to time. Certainly not her preferred type by any means, but if the occasion called for it, she'd be willing to fuck her hard until she begged for mercy.

"We'll be taking off shortly," the older woman continued, "then stopping at LAX to refuel. The flight will take us about 16 hours. Strap in!" The sun was already beginning to set over the airport terminal in the distance. Michelle was grateful for this – she would be able to sleep for part of the way there at least. There was nothing worse, in her mind, than getting to a destination feeling exhausted and unprepared for what could come next. And in her line of work, one must always be prepared for anything.

The interior of the jet was immaculately designed, with wooden finishings and large, comfortable recliner seating. There wasn't a woman alive who would pass up an opportunity to fly to the States in this beautiful beast. Everything was immaculately prepared for a Presidential guest, with pillows and blankets, and copies of risqué magazines peeking out of the pocket in the side of the chairs.

There were no other passengers other than Michelle and Charlotte, and the apparent bull dyke. Michelle followed Charlotte deeper and deeper into the cabin, taking their seats next to each other. She hadn't felt this level of comfort in a long time. It was certainly more than the Australian government could afford, though some days she surprised they didn't make her sit on an upturned tin bucket. She relaxed her whole body into the leather seats, and stretched her arms and legs in front of herself. Bliss.

The air hostess disappeared behind a curtain towards the front of the jet, leaving the two women to the privacy of their own devices. Michelle could feel a nervous excitement run through her body. There was an adventure waiting for them, one that she knew would require all of her skills and abilities to complete.

Minutes later, the plane was taxiing to the runway, and making final preparations to take off. The engines whirred into life, and the lights dimmed in the cabin. Charlotte turned towards Michelle. "Is everything ok?" she asked. "You've been quiet since the ceremony at Government House."

"I'm ok," replied Michelle, who was taken slightly aback. "I'm just keen to know what kind of deals we'll be making in Washington!" She tried to sound enthusiastic, but felt her apprehensions got the better of her. She knew Charlotte sensed this too. They remained in silence as the plane sped up along the runway, and began to ascend into the Canberra twilight.

Before too long, the plane had levelled out, and the roar of the engines quietened down enough to hear each other again. "You know," said Charlotte, with a glean in her eyes, "I should really congratulate you on your big win today." There was a mischievous grin on her lips. For a sexual beast like Charlotte Adams, this could only mean one thing.

She leaned over, and kissed Michelle on the mouth, passionately, her hand snaking erotically up the front of her blouse. With tactile deftness, her fingers slipped beneath the lacy fabric of the brassiere, and glided gently over the soft, supple skin of her breast. While she teased and tickled Michelle's erecting nipples, enjoying the quiet groans of satisfaction escaping from her lips, she used her free hand to unbuckle her seat clasp. Like the aqua foam over a waterfall, Charlotte slid to the floor, seating herself up comfortably in front of her counterpart.

Although unsure of her intentions, Michelle's pussy began to moisten in her skirt. She could see Charlotte's eyes watching the growing outline of her nipples through her blouse, glancing downwards to her not-so-secret garden. She licked her lips sensually, and glanced up at Michelle again with her deep brown eyes.

The longer she kept Michelle in anticipation, the wetter her vagina got. It was a game of strength between two – who would cave into their desires first?

Charlotte eyed off Michelle's thighs, seemingly tracing the line from knee to snatch, waiting for the opportune moment to strike and pleasure her with all the unearthly delights her mouth and lips could offer.

Suddenly, it was all too much for Charlotte, and in a swift movement, she ripped apart the buttons and clasp that held Michelle's clitoris captive. In an instant, her lips were on Michelle's pussy, kissing and licking her, lapping noisily at her moistness.

Michelle was blessed with a comparatively large clitoris. It made it easier for the men to find, but with all those extra nerve endings, guaranteed her orgasms were powerful and explosive. She groaned again, louder this time, as Charlotte worked her lips and tongue over her clitoral hood and labia, focussing on the northernmost aspects, and teasing her vaginal canal with a single finger circumnavigating the rim.

Aside from the occasional slurp, the only sound either of them made was the deep, long groans and gasps that escaped Michelle's lips.

Charlotte was so good at cunnilingus, a professional in the art of lip service. Getting eaten out by Charlotte was like getting her pussy eaten by the Archangel Gabriel himself. Michelle knew this was not an opportunity to be wasted.

Charlotte's lips were soft, and her tongue wide and wet against her vulva, and when their eyes met, Michelle released the sweetest droplet vaginal moisture she could manage. She could have relaxed there and let Charlotte bring her peacefully to explosive orgasm, drenching her larynx with her feminine emissions.

She pushed Charlotte's face out of her groin, and kissed her, as deeply as Charlotte had kissed her minutes before. She wanted her so badly, over her and between her legs, to feel her skin press against her skin, their sweat dripping down their naked bodies.

It wasn't long before Michelle had taken off Charlotte's pants, leaving both women in just their shirts and bras. Their labial lips against one another's while they kissed each other with their facial lips, like duelling swords of flesh. With a seductive grin, Michelle fell to her knees before Charlotte, praying to every god above and below, for Charlotte's fingers to pleasure her womanhood as well as her tongue could.

Her womanhood was impressive, her labia thick and juicy, and her wetness sweet and salty like ocean water dripping from her heavenly hole. Michelle opened her mouth, and with slow movements, licked Charlotte's gash from slit to clit.

Glancing up, she saw Charlotte's eyes were closed, clearly enjoying the moment. With her hand, Michelle felt her way up Charlotte's simple cotton shirt, feeling every inch of her glorious tight stomach. She grazed over her breasts with the slightest touch, and brushed her wide nipples with the pads of her index fingers. Michelle enjoyed the way Charlotte's nipples seemed to jump grow hard to her touch.

With her strong hands, Charlotte pulled Michelle up from the floor by her bra, and with a single tug, ripped the fabric from her body, leaving her completely naked. "Wait here," she whispered to Michelle. It was an instruction Michelle took as seriously as the oath of allegiance she'd sworn when hired by the Australian Foreign Minister, Christopher Wayne, all those years ago.

Charlotte made her way delicately to the curtain and pulled it open, to reveal the air hostess, sitting on her assigned seat, her earphones plugged tightly in her ears, looking rather shocked at the woman who had just burst into her quiet place with her triangular-shaped patch of trimmed pubic hair thrust into her face.

"Excuse me," said Charlotte, bending over to open a cupboard located about knee height, and flashing her inner labia in doing so. After some fiddling, she found what she was looking for, and pulled out a bottle of expensive champagne. She apologised again to the distraught air hostess, closed the curtains and walked back to Michelle, who was still standing with her breasts heaving and her pussy throbbing in anticipation.

"Let's have a bit of fun," Charlotte whispered in her ear, not missing the moment to envelope Michelle's external ear with her mouth.

With a twist and a flick, Charlotte proficiently popped the champagne cork, and ever the gentlewoman, she let Michelle have the first sip, before taking a swig herself, splashing some of the valuable golden liquid down both hers and Michelle's breasts.

She smiled a cheeky grin, as she dropped to her knees, and began to lick at Michelle's cunt again, this time pressing her tongue to her clitoris and vibrating it gently in place.

Michelle could feel the bubbles of the exquisite French drop rupture on her sensitive glans, and being at a high altitude, they seemed to erupt with greater force than expected. *Maybe I'll erupt with this much force too*, she thought. She felt each pop, and the delicate burn each one gave to her sensitive snatch. Surely the plane was flying far too high, because she was in heaven by this point. But not wanting to burst too quickly, she pulled her pussy back from Charlotte's mouth, and grabbed the bottle of champagne. She took a decent swig, then tipped some into Charlotte's open moth. Setting the bottle down, she used her now chilled hand to massage Charlotte's pussy, while kissing her deeply. The bubbles of champagne burst against each other's tongues, and Michelle was pleased to feel Charlotte's legs widen slightly, just enough for her to reach her fingers along the full length of her womanly slit.

She masturbated her, fingers gliding up and down her labial cleft, dipping gently into her vagina, slowly at first, then faster and faster. Charlotte's body writhed at Michelle's touch, twisting and turning with all the sexual energy pent up beneath her skin.

Charlotte was gasping before long, and pushed Michelle's hand away from her muff. She breathed in deep, like a minotaur ready to run down her next victim. Michelle's body was ready for whatever Charlotte decided to do to her.

With a forceful hand and fluid precision, Michelle was bent over the armrest, her inner labia exposed to the open air. She could feel Charlotte pouring some of the remaining champaign over her back, trickling down and running through the aroused, open gap and into her pussy.

Sealing off the end of the bottle, Charlotte shook it briefly, and then inserted the opening of the champagne bottle into Michelle's vaginal canal and released her grip, flushing the remaining liquid into the cavern. She pulled the bottle out, and after admiring her handiwork, Charlotte slid a finger into Michelle, followed by another, fucking her deep and slow.

Michelle had never experienced sex like this before. The champagne provided an interesting sensation to her clitoris, while the gentle strokes of Charlotte's fingers gave her deep, pleasurable sensations from her G-spot. It was the sweetest punishment, the most delicious torture she could imagine. With every stroke, she felt her body lifting higher and higher, into the divine sensations of hedonistic pleasures.

Unable to hold on any longer, Michelle orgasmed, moaning loudly at the touch of Charlotte's hand. She felt every tingle across her skin and breasts, as her pleasure ricocheted through her body.

"Your turn," she said, breasts heaving with her breath. She eyes Charlotte off hungrily, and without waiting a response, pushed her over the armrest of the chair, pussy exposed to the air, and dove on her. She lapped at her labia, feeling every fold with her tongue, tasting every drop of moistness on her lips. She suckled on her clitoris, treating it like a nipple with her mouth, stroking her gently.

Charlotte was gasping and moaning loudly. The air hostess flashed them a disapproving look, but Michelle didn't mind. It only made her more determined. She pushed her fingers into Charlotte's vagina, pulling back and fingering her powerfully. With every stroke of her arm, Charlotte's body and breasts jerked violently, until with a groan, she climaxed, pussy muscles clamping down on Michelle's finger, and a dribble of liquid oozing from her beaten hole.

"I've fucked a lot of girls," Michelle said, trying to catch her breath from her efforts, "but this is the first time anybody has tried fucking me with a champagne bottle!"

Charlotte gave a small laugh. "Yeah, that was something I learned at a sex party hosted by this news anchor in Houston. Except she couldn't get the bottle out afterwards and we had to call nine-one-one." She laughed loudly at the memory.

After climbing back into a seat, and only through sheer exhaustion, both women were fast asleep. It was only when there was a jolt and a shudder from the plane, they both woke up, still completely naked, to find themselves at LAX, arguably the busiest airport in the world.

"Best get ourselves ready for action," whispered Charlotte, kissing Michelle on the lips as she handed her broken bra back to her.

CHAPTER 2 – Fuck, or be Fucked

Day: Tuesday
Time: 1000 hours (local time)
Location: Los Angeles International Airport

The local authorities had been kind enough to set aside a private transit lounge for Michelle and Charlotte, and had even brought them complementary clothes after seeing their own garments, torn to shreds and stained with champagne. Naturally, they'd seen it all at LAX, and there were no further questions asked of them. It was a level of dignity that wouldn't have been afforded to them back home, of that, Michelle was certain. They had even been offered more champagne, despite the early hour, but both women declined to indulge themselves any further. They'd both had their fair share of the drink for one day.

"Michelle, do you know why I asked you to help me with this task?" asked Charlotte suddenly.

"No," replied Michelle.

"Well, you're the best damn negotiator I've ever come across. Some of the things we did together over the last few days – I've never seen anything like it before in my life,"

Charlotte said, with a grin. "I reckon you've got a real skill for negotiation, and, for sex."

Michelle grinned. "Well," she said slowly, "when you work for the government, you learn about getting fucked over from an early point in your career. I just learned how to fuck back."

Charlotte laughed. "Is that so?" she asked. "You certainly know how to fuck; I'll give you that."

Michelle blushed silently in her chair again. What was it about Charlotte's charms that made her act like a lovesick teenager? Of course, she had been complimented on her body and sexual performance before, but hearing it from Charlotte gave her a tingle in her replacement pants.

A television in the corner was airing some sort of American current affairs show, hosted by a young, blonde woman. Michelle wasn't paying much attention to the broadcast, but was irritated at the sound of her nasally, Texan voice nonetheless. If there was one thing in the world she couldn't stand, it was conspiracy theorists. These Americans lived in a world where they were constantly fearing invasion by Canada, or Iraq, without having the slightest bit of perspective. She was glad Charlotte was nothing like those Americans. She was thoughtful and calm, a woman of the world who was able to see beyond the confines of her citizenship.

But Michelle knew better than to air these thoughts aloud. Out here, everybody was a patriot, and every second patriot carried a gun with them at all times. Instead, she waited for the staff to stop faffing about, and leave the private lounge, so that it was only her and Charlotte who remained.

"You said yesterday you needed help closing in on a deal for the President," Michelle enquired. "I'm curious – what kind of deal?"

Charlotte cleared her throat. "Well, he's currently trying to get new gun legislation through Congress, but it keeps getting blocked by the Opposition. I'm sure he will be more than happy to tell you all about it in great detail, but just know, we are dealing with some very powerful people here. I wouldn't ask for your assistance if I didn't trust you completely."

"What kind of powerful people are we talking about?" asked Michelle, hesitating slightly. She felt uncomfortable, as though she were a rat being led into a trap.

Charlotte breathed deep for a moment, as though contemplating whether or not to reveal more. "We're not dealing with the government," replied Charlotte. "We're dealing with the people who own the government – the business moguls who have the President and most of Congress by the tits and balls. You're going to meet the most powerful people in the world over the next few days."

Michelle gulped silently to herself. She had utmost faith in her ability to negotiate, especially given her impressive sexual abilities, but to meet with the most powerful people in the world… They'd surely be trained to read and reject her manoeuvres with ease. She hoped Charlotte had a plan, because in that moment, before they'd even begun, Michelle was certain they were going to lose.

Without warning, the volume of the television suddenly increased. "We have some breaking news now, coming in live from Canberra, Australia," said the news host, pausing to hear the information being fed to her. "The Australian Government has today expelled the Ambassador for France, and the Chancellor of Germany from the country, citing, what they call 'an indecent incident'. We'll bring you more information as it comes available."

Michelle and Charlotte glanced at each other knowingly, but kept low profiles. Nobody needed to know that they were in part responsible for the two Europeans being found responsible for desecrating the Prime Ministers office. In actual fact, it was Michelle and Charlotte who had framed them in order to cover up their own crimes against the PM. It was, in Michelle's mind, better to create a minor international incident than admit to her own mistakes.

"Sorry to interrupt you, ladies," interrupted an airport maître d', "but your plane has been refuelled and is now waiting for you." Being afforded the greatest level of privacy available to them in the state of California, Charlotte and Michelle were herded through the crowded terminal towards the private gate where the Presidential jet was awaiting them.

Once on board, they allowed themselves a few moments to celebrate the deportment of the Frenchwoman and her German lover. "It worked!" exclaimed Charlotte.

"I knew it would," replied Michelle coolly.

Had it only been a few days since they'd have a four-way fuck with the exiled diplomats? Michelle recalled it fondly, seeing Charlotte in action, working at her best. The recollection was enough to give Michelle a tingle in her gash.

She was insatiable for Charlotte. Every atom in her being screamed for her, every part of her longed to be pinned down and fucked until her vagina screamed for mercy.

Unable to control herself a moment longer, Michelle gave into her lusts and kissed Charlotte deeply, her tongue reaching down to the places where hundreds, if not thousands of other tongues had gone before. The hairs on the back of her head stood on end as she touched her breasts through her new blouse.

Charlotte responded by slipping her hand into Michelle's pants and G-string, and gently rubbing her still-tender clitoris. She was delicate at first, respecting Michelle's pussy considering what it had been through, touching her until her vagina flexed and her lips became wet.

Michelle leaned back, and unzipped her pants, allowing the American full First-Class access to her landing strip and vaginal zone. She kissed her on the mouth, moaning softly as Charlotte's fingers sped up, rubbing at her most sensitive erogenous zone with vigour and passion.

She loved how women always knew where to focus their efforts, as they stroked and titillated her pussy, toying with her womanhood with their fingers and tongues. She was just an instrument, and Charlotte was the conductor. She knew every part of Michelle's body to press and stroke. Rub hard and fast, then slow down. Slide a finger between her labia, and enter her womanly cavern of delights. Of all the men and women she'd been with none of them touched her the way Charlotte did.

Sure enough, just as she was feeling her orgasm rising, Charlotte's tongue was on her clitoris, her lips kissing her vulva. When she came, Charlotte sucked her labia, drawing her ejaculate into herself and relishing in it.

Gods above and below, what had she done in her life to deserve such intense pleasures of the vaginal kind? Charlotte's hands and lips were a gift from the gods themselves, her touch as silky smooth as wine. It was no wonder she maintained such a grip over Michelle's heard, when she could make her come hard with just the flick of her tongue on her cunt.

Giving herself over to the powers that be, Michelle pulled off her blouse and bra, casting them aside, and leaving her completely naked as the aircraft sped along the runway, and left the Earth below them. Within moments, Charlotte's tongue was working on Michelle's hardened nipples, swirling around and around in concentric circles, while Michelle's hand fished through her panties, feeling her way along her folds of erotic flesh.

Michelle thanked the gods that she was multi-orgasmic, capable of climaxing multiple times in quick succession. She found it amusing that people assumed God was a man – it should be clear to anyone who'd ever brought a woman to orgasm that God was a female, and one who bestowed the power of orgasmic potential predominantly to all women.

Michelle's body swayed with the turbulence as they rose through the clouds. With her fingers, she entered Charlotte's vagina, stroking and caressing her G-spot, arousing her to the point of climax.

She gasped as Charlotte's quivering tongue rasped over her nipple, her fingers once against dancing across her pussy, inside and out. Their chests heaved in unison, as their hands and mouths worked hard, bringing one another to orgasm over and over again.

"I've got an idea," whispered Michelle, pulling her face out of Charlotte's now-dripping pussy. Standing up, she fished through the overhead locker, searching for her bag. She was five orgasms in, and with anybody else, she'd have called it a night. But with Charlotte it was different. Every orgasm burned across her skin differently. It woke up a new part of her mind, a curious part that longed for more.

Within a few moments, she found exactly the tool she was looking for – a moulded dildo.

"It's modelled off the King of Sweden's," she said to Charlotte, handing her the toy. "A gift from someone I used to know."

"Well, if it's good enough for the Queen of Sweden, it's good enough for me," replied Charlotte with a smirk, spreading her legs and opening her vaginal lips to the silicone toy.

Within seconds, Charlotte was fucking herself with the replica dildo, while Michelle sucked at licked at her nipples. She was slow and deliberate with her thrusts, undulating her body as the phallus slid in and out of her snatch. Michelle had only had the pleasure of seeing Charlotte getting fucked by a man once before, but was so turned on by the sight of her pushing the fake cock into her hungry hole. Standing up, Michelle pushed her pussy to Charlotte's face. There was no mistaking her intention.

She grabbed her breast in hand, gripping onto her own nipples as Charlotte's tongue ravaged her clit and labia. She couldn't hold on anymore, and with howls of ecstasy, the two women came harder than they ever had before. Hot gushes of orgasmic fluids erupted from their vaginas, drenching the seat beneath them.

"I think we'll need to find somewhere else to sit," gasped Michelle, now sprawled across the President's own special in-flight chair. Life couldn't get any better, she thought to herself. How many other people had fucked a local sexpert on the President's private jet before? Not many, that's for sure. She quietly wonder to herself, just how many other world leader's places of business would Michelle and Charlotte fuck each other senselessly? She couldn't wait to find out.

CHAPTER 3 – A Presidential Request

Day: Tuesday
Time: 1330 hours (local time)
Location: Washington, DC

By the time they arrived in Washington, it was already early afternoon. A black chauffeured SUV, with both Michelle and Charlotte inside, snaked its way up the drive to the White House. Michelle looked out the windows at the winter wonderland outside, the light dusting of snow on the grass and in the trees.

Despite her job and her broad experience, Michelle had never met a President of the United States before. Even so, she held some reservations about Geoffrey Nash. By all accounts, he was a megalomaniac from Texas, an oil tycoon who had profited immensely from operations in the Middle East. If rumours were to be believed, Nash bought the Presidency for the sum of $175 million dollars, small change for a billionaire like him. Others say the Presidency was bought by the Russians, and he was but a pawn in the long-standing rivalry between the two former superpowers. If other rumours were to be believed, it was the death threats his cult-like following levelled against his opponent that caused them to withdraw from the Presidential race, leaving only one man standing come polling day. There was something about the man, from what Michelle had seen on TV, that told her getting on his bad side would be the last mistake she'd ever make.

They were welcomed to the White House by the Secret Service and the President's personal body guards, six men, each of them at least seven feet tall, and dressed all in black. For a moment, Michelle wasn't sure whether to be intimidated or aroused. "Wait here," one of the guards said. "You'll need to go through the security screening." Michelle relinquished her designer handbag to the guards, and proceeded to be thoroughly examined. The man, who was African-American and incredibly attractive, started to pat down Michelle's lower body, first her right leg, then her left. He moved onto her upper body, feeling her perfectly toned abdomen, and deliberately moving his hand to meet her breast.

He wore a wry smile that said "meet me later, little lady." Of course, Michelle had been with black men before, as a rare treat, and just maybe she had another luxury coming her way.

"Well, Ms Morgan, it seems you have some interesting items in this bag," one of the guards called out, holding Michelle's bag, evidently immediately after rummaging through the contents. "I'm concerned that some of these items and unmentionables could pose a security risk to the President."

"What, a couple of dildos and a vibrator?" asked an incredulous Michelle. What a ridiculous, prudish country this was. Back home, there was a sex toy shop on every corner but here, on God's own country, it was an apparent crime to carry about a 13-inch hunk of vibrating silicone.

"We can't allow any phallic objects over 4 inches in here," replied the guard, sounding almost embarrassed. "The President views them as a threat. I'll need to keep your bag here, and you can collect it on your way out. Oh, and I won't touch your items, you can rely on me."

In an instant, it all made sense to Michelle. It wasn't a security issue per se, but an issue with the President's personal security. But, if that was the only issue they ran into while they were here, she could leave once again feeling completely satisfied.

With only minor ceremony, Michelle and Charlotte were escorted by security through the hallways and corridors, all the way to the famed Oval Office. The door was creaked open, until the President's chair – its back turned to them – was revealed.

"Mr President, sir!" barked one of the body guards. "The negotiators are here."

With dramatic flourish, the armchair swivelled around to reveal President Nash. He was a short man - shorter than Michelle expected – but was clearly well toned and in good health. Michelle estimated he was in his early sixties, judging by the greying hair that covered his head. He had a semi-handsome face, perhaps slightly better looking than the average American.

"Very well," said the President, in a matter-of-fact way. "Let's get down to business, shall we?" His tone was gruff, almost angry, but that's how he always seemed on television when he spoke. Maybe it was all an act, maybe that was just how the President was in real life. Michelle didn't know, and quite frankly, she didn't want to know Geoffrey Nash well enough to decipher between the real him and the Presidential him.

The two women were directed to two chairs, positioned perfectly before the desk, with two identical manila folders in front of each of them.

"Ladies," continued the President. "I have been informed of the excellent work you both do. Adams, you have aided me in my Presidential campaign, and…" The President paused for a moment, and looked directly at Michelle. "I have been informed you do some excellent work as well in the field of political negotiations. Now, I have important legislation to get through the Congress and you are both going to help me. So far, it has been debated on, picked at, prodded, and has still yet to pass. Now let me ask you something, Australian – what is your name?"

"Michelle Morgan, sir."

"Morgan. Well, Morgan, do you what makes America great?"

Michelle hesitated. She could tell this was a man who was quick to anger, and did not want to give him the wrong answer. "Freedom, sir."

"Freedom…" sneered the President. "Freedom? Fuck freedom!" he roared. "Freedom has gotten us nowhere! No Morgan, it's not freedom that makes America great; it's our guns. Guns make America great. Every good, true, patriotic American owns a gun. But there are those who don't own a gun. There are traitors amongst us."

Michelle wasn't sure where this was going, and gulped silently to herself again, for the second time that day. The man before him, the President of the supposed free world, looked positively maniacal. He sat in his chair, all six-foot-four-inches evident as he sprawled his body out awkwardly, grinning from ear to ear, his face a flush of red with fury. There was no telling what this disturbed metal asylum escapee would say or do next. Michelle knew in that moment, as she stared into the President's beady little eyes, that he was going to gift them with a task so monumental, it would take all of her skills – and then some – to accomplish her victory.

The President continued. "Ladies, I was elected to this great office, legitimately and without interference, so that I could do one job, and one job only – to make every American a true patriot. Mark my words, I am going to introduce legislation to force every man, woman, child and God damn foetus to own a gun. There won't be a single country on Earth with as many guns as America by the time I'm done with it."

Michelle felt the urge to point out that America already did, in fact, have the largest number of guns in the world, both in absolute terms and on a per-capita basis. Her sensibilities won out in the end, and she kept silent. Better not to give anything away, or anger the President any further.

"Open your folders, girls. It contains all the information you need to achieve your goal. I should tell you now, the information here had been collected by Americas' finest – our security agencies and intelligence communities. The information found herein is strictly confidential. Which means – you, Aussie gal," President Nash exclaimed, snapping his fingers twice trying to get Michelle's attention. "Yes, you – I don't want to hear Prime Minister What's-His-Name bringing up any of this business at the next G20, you hear me?" he demanded, his arms and hands flailing about himself for dramatic effect.

"Yes, Sir. Understood."

What was in the folder was more than Michelle had expected. It was a dossier, a detailed document containing the personal and private information of dozens of high-profile men and women. The level of detail was remarkable, from their personal particulars, their biometrics, and minutiae of any scandals they'd been involved in, all the way down to their sexual proclivities. Even the briefest of reports gave Michelle the deepest insight into the personal lives of these individuals, so much so that she felt as though she knew each of them personally. It was immediately apparent to Michelle what was to be expected of her and Charlotte – these individuals were targets, and it was their job to convince them to publicly support the President's dastardly goals.

"Where do you suggest we begin?" asked Charlotte, breaking several minutes of stunned silence.

The President paused for a moment, and looked deep in thought. He hummed a tune to himself that sounded suspiciously like a well-known children's song, as he swayed back and forth. After a few seconds, he opened his eyes and said quietly, almost a whisper, "Page 6. That's Annabeth Hanson, the owner of JF Enterprises, a publishing corporation. She is also a staunch anti-gun campaigner, and has been working against my legislation. I should have her charged with treason!"

Michelle flipped to the page, and immediately began to skim through the details provided. The provided photo, a black and white photocopied square that was clearly taken using a long-range camera lens showed a beautiful woman of forty-one, with long black hair, and a slender frame. Everything from her hairstyle to her pink designer coat screamed 'publisher'. But it wasn't her appearance Michelle was interested in; it was her secrets.

Annabeth Hanson had been an anti-gun campaigner ever since her beloved dog, a white poodle named Mrs Tipsy, was fatally shot while out for a walk in New York City's famed 5th Avenue. The assassin had yet to be formally identified, but that didn't matter to the scorned woman. One bullet was all it took for her to be converted to a radical anti-firearms activist.

She was married to a man, Monty, who was also present on the day of the shooting. And now like a pair of militant vigilantes, they used their publishing clout to actively force their point of view on the world.

Of course, Michelle viewed them as very reasonable and passionate people, but even the way the document was written made her want to loathe the very ground they walked upon. It was abundantly clear that together they'd created quite the dent in the President's plans already, and he wanted them taken out.

Looking further through her details, Michelle couldn't help but notice Ms Hanson was reportedly bisexual, and had a penchant for pre-op transgender men. Although Michelle Morgan was not one to judge – let a thousand blossoms blooms, as they say – but did wonder if these proclivities would prove beneficial or a hinderance. Bisexuals were a fickle breed by nature, keeping the mysteries of their sexualities close to their chests, until it was time to strike and take down a lover for the night. As a bisexual herself, she knew this all too well. But it was the last line on the page the grabbed at Michelle's attention. She fixated on the words until they ran through her head on a loop. *Known to frequent BDSM clubs when Monty is out of town; presumed submissive.* There, Michelle thought to herself, a satisfied smirk beginning to form on her lips. That's where they would get Annabeth Hanson.

"I think we have all the information we need to get started, Mr President," said Michelle. "We'll be in touch in the coming days to discuss our progress."

Michelle and Charlotte stood up in unison, and each shook the President's hand before leaving. They were led by the Presidential security guards back to the main entrance, where Michelle's bag was waiting for her. Once satisfied none of her important tools were missing, the two operatives were escorted back to the vehicle. It was only once they were dropped off and checked into their hotel room that Michelle allowed herself to relax. "I have ideas, Charlotte," she began. "We're going to need to work quickly at this." And with that, she began to describe her plans to Charlotte.

CHAPTER 4 – Between a Tit and a Clit

Day: Thursday
Time: 2230 hours (local time)
Location: New York City, NY

It was late into the evening when the wheels of the chartered jet came to a screeching halt on the tarmac of JFK Airport. Together, Michelle and Charlotte had spent the last two days and millions of public dollars hatching together a plan so intricate, it was guaranteed to work. All that was left to do now was let the pieces fall into place, and like clockwork, the complex machine they'd built together was set off in motion.

Somewhere on the other side of the city, Monty Hanson, the husband of their target, Annabeth, would be stepping onto a plane any moment, ready to fly to Dallas for what he thought was to be an emergency meeting of the National Poodle Committee. Michelle smiled at the thought of him presenting his case to the company of out-of-work actors Charlotte had hired to pay the role of the Committee, even complete with some borrowed poodles of their own.

As he was doing this, Annabeth would be preparing herself for a late-night party at her favourite downtown BDSM club,

Puppy Play. Gay, straight, bisexual or anywhere in between, married women were as predictable as a sunrise. While the husband was away, the fiddler would play.

As for Michelle and Charlotte, they were busy running through their final checklist, before they de-boarded the plane. "Gun-shaped dildo, bullet-shaped vibrating butt-plugs, ammunition-style nipple clamps, EZ4U Anal Lubricant," she listed, pointing to each item in Charlotte's open briefcase. It was stocked with all the essential and non-essential leather paraphernalia, classic-style whips and chains, and handcuffs to boot. Everything that would make a gun-loving nymphomaniac climax like the Great Geyser of Perpetuality.

Charlotte wasn't happy, however. They had planned to hire a sex worker from the transgender brothel, only to find none of the men available for the night were of the standard Annabeth Hanson enjoyed. In plain terms, they'd undergone the operation, and were suddenly of no use to them anymore in this scenario. It took some quick thinking, and a hasty last-minute arrangement of plans, but they found their solution. Charlotte Adams was to play the role of the pre-op trans man.

She stood there, in the hallway of the Big Surprise Brothel, all five-foot-eight of a woman, wearing a tight leather outfit and harness, no make-up on her face, and sporting a pair of glorious fuck-you-up army boots on her feet. The men at the brothel were kind enough to help out with her short, fake beak and moustache, and Michelle was impressed with their handiwork. It was like watching a thirty-something year old woman trying out as a drag king for the first time.

Not one to miss out on all the fun, Michelle was also dressed for the occasion. She checked herself out in the mirror, admiring the way her leather dress hugged her buttocks, and the corset pulled her breasts up even higher, making them spill over the top of the dress. Atop her blonde hair was a leather cap, the kind that told any potential lovers that she meant business.

"How do I look?" asked Charlotte nervously.

"Well, you look like you've got a big swinging dick hidden somewhere in your crotch!" replied Michelle, enjoying Charlotte's scowl. "Now let's get moving, it's nearly midnight, and I want to get there before Annabeth so we can stake out a location."

You wouldn't know there was a BDSM sex club there on Park Avenue, nestled in the basement of an ornate and garish church. Perhaps it was fitting that the entrance was through the rear. But they were quickly ushered into Puppy Play like they were regulars, after paying the door security handsomely to let them know when Annabeth Hanson arrived.

The club itself was dimly lit, save for some red lights dotted across the ceiling. Looking around, the whole facility had a dystopian vibe, with steel cages and torture racks scattered about the room. It reminded Michelle of the bike sheds back in school.

"Let's set ourselves up over there" said Charlotte, pointing to a dark corner in the back of the club. There was a single chair, directly below a red light, with chain fencing of the walls and a number of different tools hanging from hooks. It was perfect, exactly what Michelle had hoped they'd find to conduct their business together in the dark.

Before long, the security guard notified them that Annabeth had arrived, and was wearing an identifiable red puppy mask. With their workspace set up now, ready for action, it was time for Charlotte to work her magic. They'd rehearsed this together in the cab from the brothel to the club, but now it was 'go time'.

As soon as a woman, wearing a bright red short leather dress, with leather harness, and a bright red leather puppy mask appeared around the corner, Charlotte sprang into action. She walked over to the woman seductively, walking stiffly, like a man, in wide confident steps that would make any woman moist at the loins.

"I just love puppies," Charlotte breathed in an unnaturally deep tone. "Especially naughty ones – and you look like the naughtiest puppy I've ever seen."

Annabeth nodded.

"Would the puppy like to go for a little walk?"

Michelle was impressed by how quickly Charlotte filled in her new role of the pre-op transgender man. She was a natural actor, clearly, and gifted with the most impressive tits and clit, worthy of every Oscar nomination available.

"I see you've found us quite the naughty puppy, Darryl," Michelle said, acting up the part, as Charlotte brought Annabeth to the dark corner. "Well done, my love, my handsome, pre-op transgender husband."

This was enough to really get Annabeth's attention, and her eyes widened behind the eye holes in her mask. It was like drawing a honey bee to a rose, all they needed to do was lay out the bait.

"How should we punish this puppy?" asked Charlotte, now in a gravelly, yet still seductive voice.

"Naughty puppies get spanked," replied Michelle coolly. "Get on your hands and knees!" she barked at Annabeth, surprised to see her comply enthusiastically.

"I should let you know my safe word is 'snowflake'," Annabeth offered, on her hands and knees.

"Good to know," said Charlotte. "Lift up your dress, and I'll reduce your punishment by one spank."

Annabeth tugged at the hemline with one hand, and after a brief struggle, revealed her bare ass.

"Good puppy," breathed Michelle, and immediately began to spank Annabeth with a bare hand, not hard, but enough to soften up the tissues and increase blood supply to her buttocks, so that she wouldn't do any damage later on. When she was sufficiently tenderised, Michelle asked the all-important question – "Which side should I spank you on first, puppy?"

"The right," said Annabeth. "It deserves a bigger spanking."

Michelle and Charlotte got to work, spanking and smacking the exposed ass with their hands and a leather riding crop Charlotte found on the wall. They continued for about twenty minutes, without hearing even the barest peep from Annabeth. Michelle knew it was time to up the ante, and pulled from her bag of tricks the bullet-shaped vibrator she bought before. She turned it on, and upon hearing that satisfied buzz, placed the device against Annabeth's puppy mask so that it was on her left cheek.

"You know what this is, don't you," she whispered to Annabeth.

"Yes," the businesswoman replied.

"I think you've been sufficiently punished," said Michelle. "Would you like me to reward you for your efforts?"

Annabeth responded by thrusting her ass in the air and spreading her legs slightly, exposing her vaginal lips and pink vestibule. Michelle took that as an enthusiastic 'yes', and after lubing up the device sufficiently, began to tease Annabeth by using the tip of the vibrator on her labia. She changed the pressure and teased her further, waiting for Annabeth to beg her to penetrate her, deeply. Charlotte winked at Michelle when that request came, as the vibrator was plunged deep into Annabeth's twat, pulsating hard against her engorged G-spot.

Michelle relaxed back, listening to the sounds of Annabeth's gentle moans of ecstasy. She timed every movement of her hand with the deep inhalations of her victim's chest, pushing the vibrator in deeper, and pulling it back out again. It was all the in art of the tease. Make a woman reach the brink of the climax, and she'll be putty in your hands.

After a few minutes, Michelle pulled out the gun-shaped dildo from the suitcase, and showed it to Annabeth. She smiled to herself as her eyes went wide through the puppy mask. This was going to be psychological torture so sweet it risked putting them all in a diabetic coma.

"This might hurt, but you're going to stay quiet unless you need to say your safe word," she instructed, making sure Annabeth understood. With a flick of the wrist, and gentle corkscrew motion, Michelle pushed the dildo into Annabeth. She squirmed gently, before offering herself over completely to the feeling of the fake military-style weapon plunging into her pussy. Michelle was sure she knew what her submissive was thinking in that moment — *how could something that causes so much harm give so much pleasure too?*

For Michelle too, it was a pleasure to see Annabeth writhing about, thrusting herself back and forth, pleasuring herself against the silicone and lubricant. It amazed Michelle to no end how women would willingly give up all their closely-held beliefs for a bit of sex.

"I want you both to fuck me, hard!" gasped Annabeth.

This what the moment Michelle had been waiting for. With a wink and a nod, she turned to Charlotte, and mouthed 'your turn' to her.

Charlotte raised her fist high in the air, and with little fanfare, plunged it deep into Annabeth's perfectly lubricated cunt. The New Yorker gasped in response. She clearly didn't expect this 'trans man' to have such a dainty hand, but welcomed it nonetheless.

With a slap of skin on skin, Charlotte slapped Annabeth's buttock, and with loud slurps from the set of lower lips, moved her fist in and out of her pussy, responding expertly to her every gasp and moan. Sure, toys were good, but the real deal was always better when attached to a woman who knew how to use her skills.

Michelle kissed Charlotte deeply, working hard to ensure they reached their goal, but also not wanting to miss out on any action. There were no rules that said she wasn't allowed to enjoy herself while on a mission. Charlotte's free hand snaked up Michelle's dress, and massaged her clitoris in time with the thrusts of her fist.

When it was time to swap jobs, Michelle pushed three fingers into Annabeth swiftly, stroking her G-spot and clit, and leaned over so that Charlotte could also get involved. There was no point leaving a wet pussy unattended, not in this business. She took the hint, and pushed her clit to Michelle's mouth. Soon the sound of moans and groans filled the air, drowning out the sounds of spankings and wankings from the other patrons of the club. Michelle was fingering Annabeth as fast as she could, and knew Charlotte was matching her every move perfectly. A groan came from Charlotte's mouth and a shudder through her body indicated she climaxing, starting off the chain of orgasms. Annabeth came next, groaning and gasping with orgasmic pleasure, as Michelle quickly rubbed her own clit, bringing herself to climax in less than ten seconds.

But the grand finale, the biggest climax was yet to come. "We're not done with you yet, puppy," Michelle sneered, as she wiped the sticky vaginal secretions from her hands. "Sit!"

The pup obediently sat on the chair Michelle had pointed to, and allowed her to handcuff and chain her in place. If she was a woman who was into torture, then the next move would have her positively screaming with ecstasy.

With a swagger and a skip, Michelle pulled off the red puppy mask, to reveal the woman beneath. "Now, Ms Hanson — may I call you Annabeth?" she asked.

Annabeth's face was etched with shock in an instant. "How did you know my name? What is this? What's going on?"

"All in good time, girlfriend," cooed Charlotte, expertly removing her beard and moustache to reveal the woman underneath.

"Annabeth," started Michelle. "Annabeth, I haven't been honest with you. Behind these wires," she said, indicating the chain fencing on the walls. "Behind these wires are four cameras, that have recorded everything that happened in here just now. Everything. Now if you don't want that footage being given to Monty and the media, you'll need to comply with a few simple requests."

She raged and railed in her chair, but it was futile. The only way she'd be getting out of this mess unscathed would be to comply completely with Michelle and Charlotte's demands. "Anything," she said quietly. "I'll do anything, but please don't show my husband!"

Michelle smiled, satisfied with the answer. It was a wicked game they played, but now they'd scored the home run, the touchdown, the checkmate. There was no room for Annabeth Hanson to move, both figuratively and literally.

"You're going to tell your friends in the Congress to vote 'yes' to the President's gun proposal," Charlotte demanded, her Southern drawl more apparent than ever.

"What? No!" cried Annabeth. "Even if I asked them, they would never! They hate guns just as much as I do!"

"Well, they might change their minds after seeing you get fucked by a bullet and a gun," laughed Michelle.

"If any of them do vote against the legislation, even one of your Congress friends, this video gets leaked. Got it?" said Charlotte, clearly enjoying her 'bad cop' moment.

Annabeth looked defeated. The blood had drained from her face and she suddenly looked ten years older. She was trapped between a tit and a clit. "I'll do my best," she said quietly.

Michelle looked at Charlotte, who looked back at Michelle. They negotiated silently – believe her and let her go, or keep her a bit longer so she knew they meant business. Eventually, they agreed to release her back into the night, with one final warning.

"Remember, Annabeth – if you fail to convince your friends in Congress to vote for the President's bill, all this footage is going to shown on a billboard in Times Square. So don't fail." And with that, they undid the shackles, and she bolted from their presence like a bat out of Hell.

"That was easier than I thought it would be," said Charlotte, as they gathered their tools and most importantly, their video cameras.

But Michelle wasn't so sure, not just yet. She was just one woman, who had the power to convince three Congressmen to vote for the President's bill. But there were so many more, so many and so little time. If anything, their endeavours were only just beginning, and there was a long, long, long road ahead.

CHAPTER 5 – The Ghost of Fuckings' Past

Day: Friday
Time: 0730 (local time)
Location: New York City, New York

By the time Michelle's alarm went off, she was all stiff and sore from the previous night's adventures. She rolled around her hotel room bed, gingerly testing all her joints out. While she wasn't an old woman by any stretch, she wasn't as young as she used to be either, and at the tender age of thirty-two, she didn't bounce back as well as she would have a decade ago.

Still, her pussy remained wetter than it had ever been, and her body was phenomenal by any definition. There was nobody in the world, except for perhaps Charlotte Adams, who could do what Michelle did, day after day, night after night, clit after clit and cock after cock.

"Coffee?" asked Charlotte, offering her a mug after she emerged from her room. Michelle obliged, even though she hated American coffee and thought the only place in the world to have a decent latte was in Melbourne, or Canberra during a sitting week. It's like that old saying goes, "Melbourne for coffee, Sydney for cocktails, Brisbane for cheap drugs."

Michelle took a gulp of bitter, burnt black coffee and immediately began to regret her decision. It was a poison that flowed through her gut, no doubt causing all sorts of havoc on the way out, but it was all worth it for that rush of sweet caffeine.

"Have we decided who our next target is?" Michelle asked casually, as she drained the last of her coffee down her throat.

Charlotte handed her a copy of the manifesto the President had handed them, only a few days ago now. "Have a look," she gruffed.

With the professional dignity she'd learned during her tenure with the Australian Government, Michelle began to peruse the documents for the umpteenth time. They were all familiar to her now, every one of their targets. She knew their innermost secrets, the sorts of things nobody outside government agencies knew. Black and white faces looked back at her, as she eyed them over, selfishly deciding which ones she'd like to fuck. But it was while she was having her second look through that one particular folio jumped out at her.

"Charlotte, open to page nine – Gregory Miller, from Alabama," Michelle said, excitedly.

Charlotte opened to the page, and immediately saw what caught Michelle's eye. The file detailed Mr Miller's business arrangements, his affiliations to a number of Congress-people, and the details of his wife's fatal car accident. Included was a photo of Mr Miller's wife, Pauline, before the accident. The resemblance was almost uncanny. She looked just like Charlotte!

"Spooky, huh?" Michelle commented, comparing the photo of the dead Pauline Miller with the very much alive Charlotte Adams.

Reading further, the dossier noted that Mr Miller had been devastated by the death of his wife, driven mad by grief, and had spent the last three years of his life as an alcoholic, a shadow of a man. This was the avenue they had been searching for.

"What do you think?" asked Michelle.

"I think we're going South," replied Charlotte with a grin.

They used their time on the plane wisely, grateful for the internet access provided. Using a search engine, they found all they needed to know about Pauline Miller. There were a number of videos, including some of Pauline and Gregory together, enough that they could analyse her speech patterns and mannerisms. The plan was simple, but the task complex. In order for Charlotte to impersonate Pauline, she needed to change her speech patters for a start, switching from a classic Southern accent to something a little more rounded, which involved her losing her familiar twang. But by the time the plane landed, she had mastered the dead woman's vocal patterns, and even her facial expressions. Her hair, too, had been styled just like it was in the photo, swept to the side rather than pushed back. It was, in Michelle's opinion, nothing short of remarkable. Charlotte Adams was a master spy, someone who could even teach Michelle a few lessons.

With the transformation complete, the plan was simple. As the ride-share car pulled up outside the Yellowhammer Slammer bar, Michelle got out and walked into the bar, ordered a Cosmopolitan, before sitting at a booth next to the window.

The inebriated Gregory was sitting on a stool, slightly hunched over at the bar. He looked utterly pathetic, gurgling on a glass of scotch whisky, drowning his sorrows in this dingy hell-hole. They were about to make his life even worse than it already was, but in that moment as Michelle watched him, she wasn't sure how much worse than rock bottom he could get.

Michelle gave Charlotte the signal through the window – stroking her right eyebrow with her middle finger – and moments later she entered the bar. Charlotte, who was now playing the role of Pauline, strode over to the bar, and sat on the stool next to Gregory. For a few moments, nothing happened. But then, just as the mourning man turned to look at Charlotte, all hell broke loose.

"No, no, no! No, it's can't be," Gregory stammered, knocking his glass of scotch over. He was, understandably, in a state of pure shock after his wife, who had been dead for three years, was suddenly sitting at the bar next to him.

Michelle glanced around. It was only the three of them, four if you included the barman, so there were no witnesses around to interrupt them. The last thing they needed was some busybody coming over to find out what was going on.

"Greg, honey, it's me, really. I can only be here briefly though," Charlotte said, in perfect character.

"How? What is this?" asked Greg. "What's going on?" His mouth gaped open and closed like a catfish on dry land.

"We have some business to get to here, Greg."

Michelle watched on quietly, not wanting to draw any attention to herself. She sipped on her beer, pretending to look out the window, all the while listening in on every word that was being said.

"No, not now, not yet," Greg replied. "I haven't had a decent fuck in three years. If you really are the ghost of my dead wife, you'll let me fuck you."

Michelle froze. Sex had been their last resort to convince Gregory to do what they demanded of him, but now he was messing their plan up before they'd even started negotiating with him. It was up to Charlotte now to steer this in the right direction.

Gregory continued. "Let's go fuck in the restroom, there's nobody else in there."

With a drunken little stagger, he led Charlotte with him, past Michelle, and through the saloon doors. Fortunately for Michelle, she was able to swivel herself in such a way that she was able to see through the crack in the door, just as Greg launched himself at Charlotte, kissing her on the mouth, deeply and hard. In the grips of passion, Charlotte grasped onto Greg's firm ass, pulling him towards herself.

Michelle couldn't help herself from feeling aroused, her pussy moistening slightly in her thong at the sight of Greg pulling off Charlotte's dress, and kissing her on the chest and breasts. He worked his way slowly downwards, kissing and touching Charlotte as if to be certain she was real. When he reached her black panties, Greg used his teeth to pull them off, letting Charlotte's vagina to be exposed to him.

Was it strange, inappropriate even, for Michelle to watch her love interest seduce and fuck a man in front of her? There was nothing about the situation that felt right, but she was determined to get the job they'd been hired to do done, no matter what it took.

"It's just like I remember," gasped Greg, putting his nose to her triangular trimmed pubic hair, and inhaling deeply.

With a look of wonder and immense satisfaction, he began to lick and slurp at Charlotte's clitoris, and gently fingered her cunt.

Jealousy wasn't an emotion Michelle was accustomed to, not when it came to men and women at least. But Charlotte was a different breed. She was alluring in all the wrong ways, and even now, watching her getting eaten out by a strange man in a bathroom stall, Michelle wished it were her kneeling on the piss-soaked floor, servicing the woman who had taught her so much already.

With delicate, womanly finesse, Charlotte pulled Greg up to her, undoing to buttons on his plaid shirt one by one. She kissed him again, before undoing the button and zip of his pants, dropping them to the floor.

As Michelle watched on, Charlotte sucked on Greg's cock — tenderly at first, like she was tonguing the most delicate peach, before inhaling his manhood into her throat, and giving him the oral loving of a lifetime.

Judging by the look on Greg's face, he was enjoying every millisecond of his time, getting blown by the ghost of his dead wife. It became apparent just how much he enjoyed his time, when he pushed Charlotte against the vanity, and shoved his cock inside her, thrusting deep until he was balls-deep inside her pussy.

Green with envy, Michelle watched on as Charlotte was fucked the man, her breasts heaving with every thrust, his hand on her clitoris. She hoped Greg Miller knew exactly how lucky he was to be fucking someone as beautiful and deadly as Charlotte Adams. There was no way his dead wife would ever be able to pleasure him like that.

Charlotte moaned and groaned loudly, gasping as Gregory drove her closer and closer to climax. Her voice echoed out from the restroom, the ecstasy of pleasure evident in her cries. Still, Greg fucked her harder and harder, lifting her leg with his arm and pounding at her pussy with his sizable manhood, pummelling her clitoris with his pubic bone.

With a roar of victory, he climaxed into her, filling her vagina with his seed that dribbled out slowly when he removed his cock again.

"Do ghosts like to drink?" asked Greg, wiping himself down, and surveying the damage done to Charlotte's womanhood.

"Well, I suppose I could stay for one or two, while we get down to more important business," replied Charlotte.

Michelle diverted her gaze back out the window, as the couple walked back through the saloon doors towards the bar. They had no shame, walking about with their clothes crumpled and their hair a mess, the aromas of each other's genitals on their breaths. She had to swallow her jealousy down. It's not like Michelle and Charlotte hadn't done exactly the same before, back in Canberra, back on the flight to Washington.

"I never thought I'd see you again," said Greg. "I buried you!"

Charlotte interrupted him quickly. "Let's not dwell on that for now, I have something important I need to pass onto you, uh, from the other side."

Michelle winced internally. Could she not have found a better way to phrase it? Greg Miller might be an idiot, but surely even he would see through Charlotte's *Touched by an Angel* stunt. Although, judging by the look on his face, he was dumber than Michelle gave him credit for.

Charlotte continued. "There's currently a bill before Congress, from the President, on reforming gun laws."

Greg looked shocked, but nodded, and took a gulp of his fresh scotch, before indicating to the bartender he wanted another. "Yes, that one about mandatory arms for everyone, I know."

"It needs to pass the Congress. I can't tell you exactly why, but it needs to. You'll have to tell all the Congress-people you back that they need to pass this reform."

Greg looked puzzled. "I can't! They wouldn't go for it."

Charlotte chose her words carefully. "You are their primary source of campaign funding. I know how much money you've given them – we were married for two years, for crying out loud, I know these things," she cried. "You just tell them you'll stop funding them if they don't vote for it."

"I can't allow that; I can't allow every American to be forced to own a gun!" Greg wailed in return, so loudly even the barman looked over in shock.

"Shhh, do you want everybody to know you're drinking with a ghost? Just do it, or I won't be able to see you again. These are orders, directly from, uh, the other side."

Michelle couldn't believe what she was hearing, but even less, she couldn't believe Greg was buying it. Of course, he was an idiot who'd spent three years drinking himself into oblivion, but even so, this was getting ridiculous.

Gregory was silent for a moment, before saying quietly, "You'll never be able to see me again? Ever?"

Charlotte nodded silently, trying her hardest to look solemn.

"Ok, Pauline," he replied, glumly. "If that's what it takes, I'll do it."

"Be sure that you do," replied Charlotte. "I'll be watching." And with that, she got up and left the bar, walking outside into the wide world again. For all Gregory Miller knew, she was being beamed up right now, when in reality, she was just trudging her way back to the share car.

When Michelle joined her, only a few minutes later, they looked at each other incredulously. "I can't believe that worked!" she gasped.

"You didn't smell his breath," replied Charlotte, feigning a gag. "He's so gone, he'll believe you if you walked in there and told him you were the King of Sweden."

Michelle laughed, but her mind was already elsewhere, thinking of their next job. They were two down, and still so many to go.

CHAPTER 6 – From Queensland With Love

Day: Friday
Time: 1800 (local time)
Location: Birmingham, AL

Michelle had the good sense to allow Charlotte to find them a hotel room for the night. She was, after all, familiar with these parts of the country, and her insight into accommodations quickly proved invaluable. It wasn't long at all before they were checked into their room – a swanky, high-end suite on the 4th floor.

No sooner had they dropped their bags to the floor, had Charlotte taken herself to the shower to wash the sweat and second-hand desperation off her skin.

All alone, Michelle felt all the disappointment and pent-up sexual tension from the day. After missing out on the action, she needed to release herself, as soon as possible. While Charlotte stripped off to shower, Michelle was busy stripping her clothes from her body as well, to take care of her own sexual hunger. Her pussy was already wet at the thought of it, and she lay on the bed, on her back, her fingers slowly tracing the lines from her ass to her clit, feeling every tantalising ridge on the way.

A little gasp slipped from her lips as she allowed her hands to wonder across her body, feeling their way across her breasts and down her stomach. They slid down over her smooth labia, toying and massaging them briefly, fingering her pussy delicately. With the sound of the shower water still running, Michelle hastily pulled a girthy, realistic vibrator from her suitcase.

She plunged the vibrator into herself, enjoying the brief moments of pain as her vagina stretched open to accommodate it, followed by the glorious feeling of intense vibrations against her G-spot. She pulled the vibrator out, and plunged it into herself again, feeling every ridge and valley as it glided past her sensitive nerve endings.

Clitoris at her fingers, she writhed on the bed, bringing herself closer and closer to orgasm. The vision of Charlotte getting fucked by Greg Miller in the bathroom stall ran on loop in her head, and she pictured himself getting fucked by Charlotte's strap on dildo. Quickening the pace, Michelle's toes curled, readying herself for an almighty climax.

Suddenly, without warning, a fully naked Charlotte Adams was standing over her. "You look like you could do with a hand there," she said with her Southern drawl. She winked, and without waiting for permission, grasped the base of the vibrator in her hand, and fucked Michelle slowly with it. Leaning over, she stimulated Michelle's clit with her mouth, lapping at every droplet of feminine lubrication until Michelle orgasmed, grasping her tits and hand and moaning loudly enough to be heard all the way along the hotel corridor.

"You've been holding that one in for a while," Charlotte smiled, wiping her mouth with her arm. "Go, take a shower. I'll start working on our next plan."

With that, Michelle waltzed to the bathroom, and left Charlotte to her own devices. She trusted Charlotte's judgement completely, especially given they were on her home soil. Still, she wanted these deals wrapped up and sorted out as soon as they could. Time was money, and with the weakened American dollar, she knew she could secure a better financial deal for herself back home. This work in the United States was basically charity, a thank you gift to Charlotte for helping her secure the last details of the Trans-Global Trade Partnership.

"What about this bitch, page forty-two," said Charlotte with a grin, as Michelle returned from her shower. "I reckon you'll be perfect for this one."

Michelle walked confidently over to the table, and flipped through the folder until she found the character Charlotte was talking about. "Is this a joke?" she asked incredulously. The woman in the photos was probably in her mid-forties, and wore a cartoonishly large Akubra hat, and jet-black sunglasses on her rugged, sunburnt face. *Roberta "Gator" Hill.*

"Are you serious? She lives in Florida and owns an alligator farm?"

"Yep," replied Charlotte. "But look here, near the bottom of the page – she spent six years living in North Queensland, Australia, back in the nineties. I reckon she must love Aussies, so you're the perfect gal to take on the job."

The more Michelle studied Gator's folio, the more confused she became. Surely this woman – this lunatic really –

surely, she did not have the power to sway the minds of Congressmen. Everything about her seemed utterly deranged. There was even an incident described where she'd sent a series of threatening letters to the Queensland Premier, which ultimately resulted in her deportation from the Land Down Under.

But it was her time in Queensland that Michelle chose to focus on. She'd founded, owned, and operated one of the largest salt-water crocodile farms in the Southern Hemisphere, making millions of dollars in a short space of time. It was of no surprise to Michelle to see photos of Gator with several prominent politicians, but there was one that stood out. Standing in front of a massive sign advertising her farm was Gator, alongside Queensland Member of Parliament, Doug Perry.

Michelle knew Doug well, particularly because it was been barely a week since she'd fucked, accidentally killed, and resuscitated the morbidly obese politician. It was abundantly clear to her that there was more to the story, and she was determined to find out what.

Within minutes, Michelle was on the phone to Doug's office in Canberra. His secretary, whom Michelle had also met, answered the phone after only a few rings.

"Doug Perry's office, how may I help?" she answered with her thick Queensland accent.

"Hello, it's Michelle Morgan here, I was there last week when –"

"Oh yes, Michelle! I'll put you through to Doug. He's back in the office already, would you believe!"

Michelle waited for a few moments before Doug's voice boomed down the line. "Michelle, how the bloody hell are ya?" he asked.

"Hello Doug, I was just calling to see how you were recovering after your heart attack." Michelle knew he was a man who liked to receive all sorts of pleasantries before getting down to business, as it were. She'd learned that particular lesson the hard way.

"Michelle, it will take more than just a coronary to kill me! I'll never be able to repay you for saving my life."

"Well, Doug, here's the thing – you can start repaying me right now. I'm in the States at the moment, and I'll be flying out to Florida in the morning. I need to know all about your relationship with Roberta Hill."

Doug was silent on the other end of the phone, save for his usual heavy breathing. When he eventually began to speak, he did so very quietly, almost a whisper. "Michelle, you're asking about something from nearly twenty years ago here, mate."

Michelle was growing impatient. "I need to know, Doug. I wouldn't ask if it wasn't important. Were you in a relationship with her?"

Doug seemed to struggle for words for a few moments. His breathing hastened, and for a few moments, Michelle worried that she was about to give him another heart attack. "Yes," he replied eventually. "Yes, although it was a long time ago. Michelle, if you're going to meet her, I gotta tell ya, she's strange. Got strange tastes and desires. That's why it never really worked out well for me and her. And you know me, Michelle, usually other people's proclivities don't bother me, but Gator… She's off the fuckin' charts! And then, well she was deported, forcefully."

"What desires, Doug? I need to know this, right now."

"She's got a thing for crocs, Michelle," said Doug, lowering his voice, presumable so his secretary wouldn't hear. "Loves 'em. Loves 'em too much, I reckon. She wanted me to dress up in a croc outfit and fuck her. That's her desire."

Michelle was used to strange requests, given her line of work. She held no prejudices or judgements about the sexual needs of others. But for the first time in her career, she really hoped to herself that this negotiation would go by smoothly, without her needing to use her best tool for the job – her pussy.

"What's that look for?" asked Charlotte as Michelle walked back into the room, immediately after hanging up the phone.

"Get your laptop out," she replied. "We've got some online shopping to do."

CHAPTER 7 – Rapturous Reptilian Rootin'

Day: Saturday
Time: 1045 hours (local time)
Location: Orlando, FL

Michelle was sitting on the bed of her hotel suite in sunny Orlando, while Charlotte was busy on the phone, talking again to one of her many connections. Michelle was still puzzled about where to find a croc outfit to seduce Gator with. They'd spent the majority of their evening in Birmingham, and the early morning flight to Orlando looking for one to no avail.

She watched on nervously as Charlotte paced around their room, her phone held to her ear in a last-ditch effort to find the sexy costume they required. They'd come so far already, too far to give up now. She was an excellent negotiator, and an even better lover, but even Michelle had her limitations. She knew her natural charm and sexuality wouldn't be enough to seduce this creep, not by a long shot.

When Charlotte finally got off the phone, she had a big grin on her face. "You won't believe it!" she cried, punching towards the ceiling. "That was just an old buddy of mine, owns an escort agency in Orlando now. They send escorts over to

Gator's place every few days, wearing the croc outfit he had made especially for their number one client!"

Michelle wasn't sure whether to feel relieved, or disturbed. It was one thing to have a kink, but to force a sex work agency to have garments custom-made was something else entirely.

Charlotte continued. "And you're in luck. They were going to send someone over this afternoon, but now, you're going in their place. Undercover. And you'll be wearing the croc outfit. Don't worry, he said they spray it down after every session, so you'll be fine."

With a few hours to kill, Michelle took herself downstairs to the hotel gymnasium. She needed to be prepared for anything, and the best way to prepare the mind was to prepare the body. After forty-five minutes of core strength training, and another half-hour of upper-arm resistance, she returned to her room, reinvigorated and revitalised.

"Look at you, all hot and sweaty," cooed Charlotte, looking up from the open dossier on the table in front of her. "It's kinda tuning me on."

"No way, not now, not when I've got work to do." Michelle felt crestfallen. She did want to fuck Charlotte, who happened to be one of the best screws of her life. But they had a job to do, and in the business of negotiations, work always came first. They'd just have to fuck later. "Anyway, I need a shower."

"Just don't be in there forever," shouted Charlotte as Michelle walked out of the room. "We've gotta get you to the agency for three! Apparently, it takes them a bit of time to get you prepared."

Charlotte's friends at the agency were kind enough to send a car to collect their newest workers. Michelle had just finished re-shaving her landing strip when the call came up from the lobby, telling them their ride was ready and waiting for them.

Although it was only a few minutes by car to the escort headquarters, it was a stifling and hot drive. This particular agency had clearly spent all of their profits on a sexy alligator suit for one particular client, rather than investing in a car with air conditioning. Michelle could only imagine what sort of people operated this business. But she didn't have to wait too long.

As the car rolled up to what could only be described as a weatherboard and iron shack in the middle of a palm plantation, a man walked out, his arms outstretched.

"Charlotte, baby!" he boomed. "I didn't think I'd be seeing you so soon."

"David," replied Charlotte, as he exited the vehicle.

He was a man of average height, but very slim, and balding. It was as though he'd lived his whole like looking youthful, and now age was starting to catch up with him, although he hadn't developed any wrinkles just yet.

"And this must be your associate," David said, turning to Michelle and shaking her hand. "Or should I say, your very *beautiful* associate."

Michelle introduced herself politely, but in the back of her mind, wondered what kind of people Charlotte was in cahoots with. The escort manager seemed utterly bonkers. Even the wild expression on his face suggested he'd been up all night, wired on caffeine or something stronger.

"I'll be turning you into an escort today," he continued gleefully, leading Michelle and Charlotte inside the smallish hut.

What couldn't be seen from outside was how elaborately decorated the inside of the building was, nor how far it stretched back. Drapery clung to every wall, dividing the building into various cubicles and booths, each layered with cushions and throw pillows. It reminded Michelle of her time in Morocco, at a local rug market. They were very quickly led upstairs to a small office the overlooked the entire palm plantation.

Sitting down at the table, David began to run through what was expected of Michelle. "Alright, let's get things started, shall we? Now, if you're in the same business as Charlotte here, you'll have no problems in the department of sex, am I right?"

"She's the best in the business," replied Charlotte matter-of-factly, giving Michelle a sly wink.

David smirked. "I could tell just by looking at you. But I doubt you've come across a client like Roberta Hill before. She's an oddity in this world. But you needn't worry – it's all above board here.

"The thing is, she won't be having sex with you, specifically. She'll be having sex with the croc costume. There's an attachment that goes on it, a vibrator or dildo or sorts – she just wants you to make the noises as if you were having sex. Sometimes she'll ask you to take the helmet off and lick her pussy a bit, but that's as 'hands on' as it gets."

"Oh, well that doesn't sound too bad then at all," said Michelle, instantly relieved. She'd had far worse experiences in her time, from far worse people. Letting someone fuck a crocodile dong strapped to her body was the least of her worries.

"But we'll need to make sure this looks like a regular job, nothing funny," interjected Charlotte. "I don't want her getting too suspicious from the start. So, I'll be staying back here and David will be going with you. Michelle, you need to give her the best croc-suit sex of her life, and then get her to agree to support the President's gun legislation."

Michelle nodded in agreement. This was a job best done solo. She had all the expertise and finesse to pull off something as simple as costumed sex.

The conversation was interrupted by the arrival of the croc costume being carried up the stairs by three burly-looking men. It was an actual, crocodile leather garment, retaining the overall shape of a croc, complete with a crocodile head helmet.

"Is that… real?" Michelle asked.

"What is real?" mused David philosophically. "Oh, the suit? Yes, it's real croc leather."

Michelle shuddered slightly. She was going to be trapped inside an actual crocodile, one of the worst fears for any Australian. Still, she'd promised she'd be willing to do anything to get this deal finalised for the President, even if that meant donning a croc suit.

Taking a deep breath in, Michelle allowed the three burly men to dress her in the suit, snapping locks shut and clicking latches into place. The only space she could see out of was a small opening where the mouth was. She was, however, delighted and surprised to find the limbs move freely in all directions. If she wanted to, she could have even tap-danced her way into Gator's farm.

As she looked down, she could see the vibrator protruding from the front of the costume, long and purple. "Oh, I thought it would be made from croc leather too!" she exclaimed, relief on her obscured face.

"No, we tried that for a while, but the leather kept falling apart," one of the burly men replied.

"I reckon she's got a pussy full of acid," added a second burly man.

"Ready to go?" asked David, an odd expression on his face, as though he were holding in a fart.

"Ready as I'll ever be," replied Michelle, her voice muffled by the costume. She closed her eyes, and hoped for the best. That's all she could do in these trying times.

She was very quickly surprised by how much one woman could sweat. It was like an oven in that suit, roasting her slowly in her own perspiration. The more she sweated, the hotter it got, until she was certain she'd die of dehydration in the hour it took them to drive to the alligator farm.

Gator was already outside, anticipating the arrival of her bi-weekly croc fuck. Through the mouth slit, Michelle could see her, standing legs spread wide apart, her ridiculous Akubra hat on her head. She looked like a caricature cowboy, or heiress to a mining corporation. How she managed to run a multi-billion-dollar empire was beyond Michelle's comprehension.

"Ya got a new one for me!" yelled Gator in a Southern drawl, as David allowed Michelle out of the car. "Taller than the others. I like that. What's ya name, girl?" she asked.

Michelle was surprised to be called 'girl'. She was, after all, thirty-two years of age, and definitely not someone many people would call 'girl'. "I'm Michelle," she replied.

"You're Australian!" gasped Gator, surprised.

A moment of uncertainty passed before Michelle answered. "Um, yes, I am."

"I spent some time up in Brisbane and North Queensland about twenty years ago now. Haven't heard an Aussie accent since I left. Where 'bouts are you from?"

"From Sydney, working in Canberra, and occasionally Melbourne for work."

"Alright, yeah, one of those Commie latte-sippers are ya? Anyway, let's get to it. Haven't got all day." Gator ushered Michelle inside, and away from David and the car. "Now I bet those jerks at the agency told you all this nonsense about me fucking my 'gators and shit, yeah?" she said, as soon as they were out of earshot of the agency owner.

"No, not at all!" Michelle replied. She didn't know what sort of situation she'd been brought into, but she knew she wanted out of it as soon as possible.

"Oh good. Some people get a bit confused by my proclivities, you know?"

Michelle certainly did not know. She'd never met a croc suit fucker in her life, and if she had it her way, she wouldn't have been near Gator in the first place.

Before she could respond, Gator had already stripped right down, and stood completely naked. Michelle was surprised to see a healthy pair of tits on her chest, and a completely shaven map of Tasmania. For some reason, she assumed a woman who wanted to fuck a crocodile suit would have some sort of deformity to her nether regions, possibly as a result of getting to close to her beloved reptilians. Gator was very well toned for someone in her mid-forties, and Michelle could clearly see that wrestling alligators all day gave her quite a work-out.

"I love a nice Aussie sheila," Gator said seductively, almost purring at Michelle. "How 'bout you take that mask off and come lick my gash?"

She obliged, removing the helmet completely, and allowing Gator to see her beautiful face properly for the first time. But it was only momentarily before Michelle set to work satisfying the businesswoman's clit with her mouth. Gator groaned as Michelle expertly licked and sucked every inch of her cunt.

"They finally got some good quality meat at that agency," Gator mused.

Michelle would have agreed, but she had her mouth full, so instead just licked more enthusiastically. This drove Gator wild, and she moaned so loudly, Michelle was certain David would hear outside in the car. Gator pulled her snatch zone away from Michelle's mouth, and slapped her breast against her face, with a loud thwack, before repeating on the other side.

Michelle got to work sucking on Gator's tits and nipples, while fingering her moist vagina with her hand, feeling her way across every labial fold. After a few moments, Gator put her hand under Michelle's chin, indicating to her to stand up fully.

"You know Michelle, I usually prefer the company of reptiles. But today, I'm in the mood for a bit of Aussie company. Why don't you take off that costume, and we can fuck the way women were made to."

Michelle obliged, and with a little help from Gator herself, the suit came apart and fell to the floor. Gator gasped at the sight of this Aphrodite who had emerged from her leathery cocoon. Greedily, she eyed off Michelle's breasts, stomach and cunt.

Without warning, she got down on her hands and knees, and welcomed Michelle's clitoris into her mouth, slurping up the single droplet of feminine moisture that glistened from the exposed, secret garden of unearthly delights. She wasn't an expert, far from it, but it was clear to Michelle that the woman was an enthusiast at cunnilingus, and it was the spirit that counted.

With a snaking hand, Gator curled her arm around to Michelle's rear, and fingered her vagina from behind with impressive dexterity. It only took mere moments for her to locate Michelle's G-spot, tapping at it and stroking it with her fingertips.

She couldn't help but let out a moan of pleasure as Gator's other hand reached up to grope Michelle's breasts, feeling for her rock-hard nipples.

When the time came, Gator pushed Michelle backwards onto the table in the room, spreading her legs far apart. There was no mistaking the alligator farmer's intentions, as she removed the vibrator, and inserted it slowly into Michelle's open hole.

She began slowly, teasing her by pulling the sex toy out, and with slow thrusts, delved it in all the way as far as it would go, before withdrawing again. Michelle gasped quietly to herself. Gator kept this up for five or six minutes, then went in hard, like a jackhammer, pounding Michelle in every direction, punishing her pussy with the vibrator. She groaned loudly, lost in the pleasures of the moment, as Gator's silicone prick send powerful vibrations through her vagina and clitoris.

She was unrelenting, too, fucking Michelle with all the force and vigour of a woman half her age. She pulverised Michelle's snatch, slamming the toy into her and attacking her with violence most erotic.

Michelle couldn't take it anymore, and gasped "Stop," before pushing Gator to the floor. It was a fuck of be fucked world out there, and Michelle needed to show this herpetophile that she was in total control of the situation. With a fire in her eyes, Michelle pulled the vibrating hunk of silicone from her vagina, and thrust it deep into Gator's begging hole.

Gator's thighs widened, exposing every part of her womanhood to Michelle. She leaned over, and suckled tenderly on her aroused clitoris, driving her even more wild. For a woman who had a thing for crocodile suits, she sure knew how to take a vibrator like a real woman. She was a woman of many secrets, and Michelle knew her sexual abilities were only the beginning.

Not satisfied yet, Michelle slapped Gator on the pussy, forcing the vibrator into her cervix and beyond. The beast bellowed with pleasure, as Michelle pounded her pussy into obliteration.

Gator couldn't take anymore, and orgasmed violently, groaning and shuddering as she squirted all over the table and onto the floor. Michelle rubbed her own clit with her hand quickly, climaxing and shirting her own juices onto Gator's bald cunt.

"There's a… there's a shower if you wanna… clean yourself off," Gator stammered, pointing to a door.

Michelle agreed she should shower, there would be too many questions back at the agency if she went back in this state. She got up, and wandered off to shower and cleanse her soul.

When she came back, she promptly put the croc costume back on, and sat down, dignified once more, at the table where Gator was reading a newspaper. "Gator, we have some business to get to," Michelle said. She continued before Gator could reply. "The President has a bill before Congress, requiring mandatory gun ownership for every American. We need you to tell the Congress-people you support to vote in favour of this bill."

Gator looked shocked for a moment, then started speaking. "I hate that damn President. He's anti-gator, that's what he is! But I love guns more than I hate that President… Michelle, I'll support this bill, but it's the only time I'll support anything that son of a bitch does in office."

"Thank you, Gator, you really are making the world, and my fuck hole, a better place." And with that, Michelle gathered herself, and walked outside, her head held high and her heels higher, back to the car where David was waiting.

"You're going to want to call Charlotte. She's got some sort of emergency happening," David said sternly, handing Michelle his phone.

She began to panic slightly. Was she hurt? Had something happened to their plan? Her fingers shook slightly as she tapped out Charlotte's number. She hadn't come this far to give up now. After three rings, the phone was answered, to Michelle's relief.

"Michelle?" Charlotte answered. "We've got a problem. Our next target… he's dead."

CHAPTER 8 – Fun at a Funeral

Day: Saturday
Time: 1630 hours (local time)
Location: Orlando, FL

"Dead?" replied Michelle. It was one thing for her to use her best tool for the job – her pussy – to negotiate with living people, but she would not fuck a corpse. There were lines of decency and standards that Michelle wouldn't cross, no matter the cost.

"John Campbell. He died a few days go," said Charlotte. "Shot while crossing the street. They're saying it was a random drive-by shooting, and he was just in the wrong place at the wrong time. The funeral is tomorrow, in Chicago."

Michelle was speechless, unsure of what her next move would be. Her mind ran at a million miles an hour. How was she supposed to turn this around now, and work to gain the support of the Congressmen in John Campbell's pocket now? But rather than giving up, Michelle knew they had to attend that funeral, and hope for an opportunity to present itself.

"Have you got a plan at all?" asked Michelle.

"I think it's best we just go to Chicago and hope for the best," replied Charlotte. "I've already ordered an 8pm flight."

Michelle thought about it for a moment. This would give them time to arrange suitable attire to attend a funeral for the billionaire media mogul. "I'll be back at the agency in forty-five minutes, we can talk more there," said Michelle, hanging up the phone. She felt it was the longest three-quarters of an hour of her life. There was a blatant cruelty to coming all this way, putting in all this effort, for it to fall apart now. Of one thing she was certain, though – she would give everything she had to get the job done.

Michelle was not in the mood to have sex with Charlotte on the flight. Besides, it was a commercial flight and there were other passengers on board. Instead, they sat in silence, each pondering their own next moves. She refused to give in to the feeling of despair. Where there was a will, there was always a way, and a way was all she needed.

The flight took 2 hours and 55 minutes, with minimal turbulence, and they arrived in Chicago at 10.05pm, local time, due to the time difference. It was 11.32pm by the time they reached their hotel, and Michelle was far too exhausted, especially after her physically draining day, to engage in extra-curricular sexual activity with Charlotte. She curled up in bed, and was asleep in minutes.

The next morning, the mood had lifted. Michelle was feeling optimistic again. They'd both run through a number of different scenarios, playing out quick scenes across the table as they ate their breakfast of bacon and eggs on toast. It was a funeral that would be attended not only by close family and friends, but also members of the Congress, politicians, and media personalities too. Together, they agreed to go after the biggest fish, go in blind but go in hard, and pick them off one by one. It would take all of their skills, both sexual and mental, and plenty of stamina to boot.

Once dressed and ready, and looking sorrowful, Michelle placed a call to the hotel reception, requesting a taxi come to collect them. While she didn't like the idea of going into a situation blind, or needing to rely so heavily on her improvisation skills, Michelle knew with Charlotte by her side, there was nothing they couldn't achieve together.

The church was still mostly empty when they arrived, save for a few guests, a Reverend, and the coffin that carried to corpse of the recently deceased John Campbell. But even as they entered the hallowed building together, every pair of eyes in the room fixated upon them. Michelle's heart rate rose suddenly. How did they know they weren't welcome here? There must be hundreds, if not thousands of people who would be in attendance. Surely, they hadn't been picked out already!

The Reverend, dressed in his ghostly robes, glided along the aisle, walking with purpose directly towards Michelle and Charlotte. A deep sense of panic, and the desire to run filled Michelle's body, but she kept her ground. If it came down to it, she'd even give the Reverend a quickie in the rectory to keep him on their side.

"You must be Mr Campbell's daughter and only living relative!" cried the Reverend as he approached the two women. "I thought you were in rehab and wouldn't be attending the funeral?"

"Uh, yes, well, I'm here now," said Michelle, doing her best to put on a Chicago accent. "Wouldn't miss it for the world."

"I'm sorry for your loss, but relieved you made it," the Reverend said solemnly. "Grief can be powerful, especially when we don't have the chance to say that final goodbye. I'll be sure to give you an opportunity to speak. Your father was very popular, and I expect it to be quite a turn out."

The Reverend ushered Michelle and Charlotte to the front row, and offered them a prime seat, where they wouldn't miss out on any of the action. In hushed tones, Michelle whispered in Charlotte's ear. "Do I really look like his daughter?"

Charlotte shrugged. "I don't know what his daughter looks like. But isn't a strange coincidence we're both getting confused for other people?"

Michelle didn't want to dwell on it. Not when she knew she'd be called up to speak at any moment now. Her hands trembled slightly as she tried not to think of the thousands of eyes on her, waiting for the moment someone yelled 'imposter', and have her thrown out of the service.

Nevertheless, an opportunity had presented itself, just as she'd hoped it would, and before long, she had dozens of ideas circling in her head. She had one chance, only one prospect at turning this potentially catastrophic situation on its head, and claiming victory.

As the Reverend approached the pulpit to speak, Michelle looked around to see the cathedral completely filled with unfamiliar faces, and a number of celebrities and dignitaries. John Campbell truly was a giant in his industry, and it was only natural for people to want to pay their respects to him.

For the next half an hour, the Reverend and others spoke of John's legacy, his generosity, and his tenacity. Of course, Michelle knew all of this information from the dossier President Nash had provided them with. Oddly enough, there was no mention of John's penchant for imported sex workers, or the fact he had three illegitimate children that he'd refused to acknowledge as his own.

Then, it was Michelle's turn to speak.

"I'd like to welcome to stage, Mr John Campbell's daughter, last remaining relative and heir to his business and vast fortune, Ms Becca Campbell," said the Reverend from the pulpit, nodding his head towards Michelle.

Michelle walked to the stage, took her place at the microphone, and began to speak. "As many of you are aware, I've spent the last several months in rehab for my sex, drug, alcohol and gambling addictions."

The crowd murmured quietly at this shocking confession. It was an unconventional way to deliver a eulogy, but Michelle didn't mind – it wasn't really her father who had died, and she didn't care whose reputation she tarnished.

Michelle continued. "My father, John, came to visit me the day before his fatal shooting, and he spoke to me about guns. He said to me, 'Becca, guns don't kill people – people kill people, and if everybody had a gun, nobody would be killed!' My father didn't own a gun personally, but I believe if he did have one, he'd still be alive today. My father told me he was going to support the President's bill to make gun ownership mandatory, for protection!"

The crowd murmured again, louder this time. In the space of a minute, this funeral had been turned from a solemn affair, to a political rally.

"And," Michelle continued, hoping not to overdo it, "As sole heir to his company, I agree completely with him. So, I ask, here, at my own father's funeral, for the Congress to pass the President's gun legislation, so that more men like my father – like John Campbell – won't be killed simply because they were defenceless." Michelle stood back and took her seat at the pew. She knew she had pulled that off expertly, without even needing to fuck anybody! She was glad for that. Even expert negotiators like Michelle Morgan needed a rest from time to time.

"Well done," whispered Charlotte.

"Do you think they bought it?" asked Michelle, earnestly.

Charlotte shrugged. "Time will tell."

The remainder of the funeral was a tame affair. Michelle did her best to appear devastated beyond belief as photos of the strange man played on a slideshow, set to music by a band she'd never heard of before. She nodded her head in agreement with all the platitudes and statements of adoration people threw for the dead man, and placed her hand to her breast as they wheeled the coffin out, signifying the end of the proceedings.

"Let's get out of here," Michelle hissed at Charlotte, before they could be interrogated further. But without even making it to the aisle, she was stopped in her tracks by on older man, African-American, and at least in his late seventies.

"Becca Campbell," he said, "Rowan Sherry, Congressman. I'm so sorry for your loss. Your father was a big supporter of mine and donated a lot to my campaign funds. Hearing what he said to you, well, I feel it is only right to support his wishes, and demand a gun-filled future for America! And I trust that you'll also be keeping up with the donations."

"I'll make you a deal," replied Michelle, using her expert negotiation skills. "I'll donate three hundred and fifty thousand dollars to your fund on the day you vote for the President's bill in Congress. And that goes for all the Congress-people my father supported over the years."

Rowan appeared very pleased with that arrangement. "You have my word, Ms Campbell."

Michelle was relieved. She could not believe her luck! They were so close now, and had almost secured all the numbers they needed for the President's bill to pass the Congress. And after that, she could be on her way back home for a much-needed rest. Finally, she felt like they were at a point where nothing could go wrong. After all the effort they'd put in, the payoff was just around the corner, so close she swore she could almost taste it. But fate has a funny way of derailing even the most well-thought-out plans, leading them into chaos and destruction…

CHAPTER 9 – Confessions in Seattle

Day: Sunday
Time: 1400 hours (local time)
Location: Chicago, IL

"Michelle, you're not going to like this news," said Charlotte, glancing up from the folder the President had given her. "Our last one, the last target – he's a man. And he's gay. We're not going to be able to fuck ourselves out of this one." She sounded crestfallen. They had come so far, only to be pipped at the end.

Michelle began to read the page for herself. Mathias Hinglebert, 43, CEO of a nationwide security company based in Seattle. In the last election campaign, he donated over seven million dollars between five congress-people. There was no way around this one. "We should make our way to Seattle anyway," said Michelle. "I completed a job like this in Germany a few years ago; we can use the same strategy and tweak it a little bit. Tell me you have contacts in Seattle?"

"I have a few, yes," replied Charlotte, suspiciously.

"Good. Touch base with them. I want to meet with them this evening. I'll arrange flights."

Michelle immediately set to work, making calculations and designing a fool-proof plan. This was the moment she needed so desperately. With limited time up their sleeves, Michelle knew there was no room for error whatsoever. She continued analysing the situation for the duration of their four-and-a-half-hour flight to Seattle. Everything they'd worked towards now came down to this single moment in time.

It was just after 9pm when they arrived at the Regal Hotel in Seattle, to find a kerfuffle happening in the hotel lobby. Michelle quickly assessed the situation, and determined that whatever had happened was already over. A man in hotel staff uniform sat on a red velvet seat in the hotel lobby, holding a white cloth up to his profusely bleeding head.

"Unhappy guest," explained the receptionist. "Asked for French champagne and was given Australian prosecco instead, so they threw the bottle at the bellboy. Don't worry, it happens all the time!" she said politely with a smile.

Shortly after checking in, four of Charlotte's contacts had turned up. Each of them had thick Russian accents, and looked like they'd been cloned in a laboratory. "When you want the best, you need a Russian," Charlotte explained to her. "Those guys will do anything for the right fee. Anything."

The group spent several hours in the hotel suite, working through all the major and minor details of the plan, role-playing and replanning until, finally, they were all satisfied with the outcome. It was the most cunning plan Michelle had ever been part of, one guaranteed to open her eyes and blow her mind when she saw it all come together in action.

"Get some sleep, boys," Michelle said eventually. "We've got a big day tomorrow. We meet at 9am sharp!" And with that, the group disbanded, allowing Michelle and Charlotte to turn in for the evening, without prying ears listening to their private conversations.

"You think you can negotiate this without using your best tool for the job – your pussy?" asked Charlotte.

"I don't just think, Charlotte, I know," said Michelle, with confidence.

"I wouldn't trust anybody else to pull off a job like this," said Charlotte, pulling down Michelle's ruby red G-string, exposing her genital area. She didn't wait for another word from Michelle before wrapping her tongue around Michelle's soft, yet still seductive womanhood, licking her gash until she was moist. Michelle moaned softly, enjoying the attention she was receiving. She closed her eyes and lay there, relishing the moments, and relaxed. She could feel Charlotte's hands reaching up her torso, feeling her ample breasts, and stimulating her aroused nipples.

With a manoeuvre, Charlotte pulled herself up the length of Michelle's body, and lay atop her, their wet pussies pressed against one another as they writhed as one on the low-thread count cotton sheets. The one constant that remained throughout this jaunt was Charlotte's insatiable desire for Michelle's body.

"Michelle, I need to say something, or confess something to you," Charlotte said, looking Michelle directly in the eyes.

"Oh?" asked Michelle, feeling a little disappointed she hadn't had her promised climax yet.

"I've enjoyed these last few days with you. A lot." Charlotte continued, looking down. "I've never met anybody like you before – smart, attractive, and a real good fuck. I think I'm falling for you, but I know you don't have time right now for someone like me, and I have a job coming up in Europe, and it could be a long one. We might not work together for a while."

Michelle sat up, and kissed Charlotte on the mouth. "I think you're great," she said. "More than great, Charlotte, I really like you. But you're right – we are both busy. It is the nature of the business we are both in. But let's not let that get in the way of things right now. Let's have sex, and then we can decide where we are at later on."

Michelle pushed Charlotte backwards, and straddled her, allowing Charlotte's fingers to find the entrance to her hole, and opened for entry. They fucked each other, caressing and stoking one another until they climaxed simultaneously. Exhaustion hit her like a bullet train, and within minutes, Michelle was fast asleep, dreaming of what life could be like for her and Charlotte if they ever ended up together.

The scene was set, ready for action. It was barely past nine in the morning, and each of the cast – Michelle, Charlotte, and the four Russians – took to their assigned positions, awaiting show time. Michelle had already been in contact with Mathias's secretary, and had set up a morning coffee meeting in a local café. It was there, they would stage their most daring act of all. The café was quiet, and that suited Michelle perfectly. Mathias was yet to arrive. When he did, several minutes later, Michelle recognised him immediately. His hair was cut into a short silver buzzcut, and his suit screamed 'fabulous but deadly'. He was everything Michelle expected him to be.

"Mr Hinglebert," she said, extending her hand out to greet him. "I'm Becca Campbell, and this is my body guard," she said, gesturing towards Charlotte. You may not know me, but I'm sure you knew of my father, John Campbell."

"Oh, yes," he replied warmly. "Yes, I did hear about his passing."

"Truly tragic," continued Michelle. "The police are still investigating his murder, but I'm not taking any chances. I've just taken over as CEO of Campbell Corp, and I need security to protect our 18 offices in the US. It would mean a big contract for you, and of course, I'd be willing to pay a premium, given the high risk involved."

Mathias pursed his lips for a few moments as he mulled the offer over. "It is certainly tempting. I can go back to the office and see if there –"

Before he could finish his sentence, loud gunshots were fired outside. This was where Charlotte's contacts came in. Two of them were outside, making all the noise, while two of them were planted inside the café. Mathias looked terrified, and the blood had drained from his face. The two contacts inside the café ran out, and each of them pulled a gun out of their pockets, and fired at the assailants, stopping them dead in their tracks. Of course, the bullets were blanks, and the wounds on the assailants were simply blood packs, but Mathias was not to know that.

"Run," yelled Michelle to her. "We'll go to your office right now, just run." And the three of them ran out of the café, and several hundred metres up the road to Mathias's building. They entered just as the building went into lockdown.

"Thank god for those two armed citizens!" gasped Charlotte. "Without them, who knows what kind of shape we'd be in!"

Michelle nodded in agreement. "This is what my father said to me just before he died – we need to arm our citizens for protection! All citizens need to be armed." She turned to Mathias, and continued. "Don't you worry, I've already been in contact with some Congress-people, and they have agreed to support the President's bill to arm all citizens, just in case…. Well, in case this sort of thing happens!"

Mathias looked perplexed, but relieved. "I've also got some people in Congress I keep in contact with," he said. "I'll get in touch with them today, and I'll urge them to support the bill. They won't say no after I've told them about what just happened."

"Good to hear," replied Michelle. "It's been a shocking morning; there's no need for us to focus on work for the moment. I'll be in contact in the coming days to arrange for security, but until then, take care." And with that, Michelle and Charlotte left the building.

"Now that we've successfully got all five on board, I think," said Charlotte, "we should celebrate with champagne." Michelle agreed with her. After the last few days, she definitely deserved a drink. Upon arrival at their hotel, Charlotte ordered three bottles of their finest champagne to their room. "Bill it to President Nash's office," she said, before waltzing off.

CHAPTER 10 – Saints and Sinners

Day: Tuesday
Time: 0600 (local time)
Location: Seattle, WA

Michelle was awoken early, at 6am, by her phone ringing on the bedside table. It was the President Geoffrey Nash calling, personally.

"Hello," she said, groggily, after her and Charlotte's drunken night together the night before. She could recall them drinking bottle after bottle of expensive French champagne, while intermittently fondling and fucking each other all over their hotel suite.

"Morgan, it's President Nash here. I'm calling you from a secure line. Listen, we've just done a quick tally of Congresspeople voting on the bill tomorrow, and I'm still down by one. This will all go to hell if you can't convince the last one to vote in favour of my bill. And Morgan – I can't afford to lead a defenceless, unarmed America. I need you to do this last job for me – or else!" And with that, the President slammed the phone down, and the line went dead.

Dead like I'll be if this vote fails tomorrow, thought Michelle with a gulp. She contemplated waking Charlotte up, but decided to leave her be. Instead, she rose, and pulled out her folio and began to skim through for possible options. She knew there would be at least one Congressman or Congresswoman who could be persuaded to vote for the President's gun legislation. It took several minutes of flipping continuously before she found a suitable candidate for her plans. And the best part – he was right in Seattle, right under their noses. Staying right in the same hotel as them. Michelle recognised him as the man who had thrown a bottle of Australian prosecco at the bellboy's head, and thought to herself *this might not be so easy after all.*

When Charlotte woke up, Michelle explained to her the situation at hand. Given their extremely limited time, they both reasoned this was their best option, especially given they did not want to annoy the President again. They spent most of the morning planning their best way to go about negotiating with the Congressman, until eventually, they settled on an arrangement. Within an hour, Michelle and Charlotte were waiting in the hallway, outside the Congressman's room, dressed in black attire, complete with black balaclavas.

Charlotte knocked on the door. "Hello," she called out, "French Champagne delivery for Senator Danube."

The door creaked open, and an older gentleman, perhaps around 84 years of age, opened the door. He was shorter than the average male, with a rounded face, clearly weathered over time. His mouth puckered up impressively, so that it looked as though it was an allograft from him own anus.

"What the –" he started. He didn't finish his sentence, because Charlotte had hit him over the head with the champagne bottle, knocking the Congressman out cold.

"See how he likes being hit in the head like that! I hope that hurt him as much as he hurt the bellboy," Charlotte said, before walking through the door, and dragging the limp man to a chair. Together, they propped him up, and using handcuffs from Michelle's bag of tricks, tied him to the chair. Charlotte shook up the bottle of champagne, and popping the cork, sprayed Redmond Danube – or Red Danube, as he was more popularly known – with the warm bubbling liquid. He woke immediately, and he did not look happy.

"What the bloody fuck do you two think you're doing? I am a Senator!" he roared.

"Shut up," said Charlotte simply. "Just shut up, old man. We'll do the talking here. We are here on behalf of the President. He has his new gun legislation tabled for tomorrow, and we want you to vote yes to it."

Senator Red Danube looked livid, living up to his name. His mouth puckered for a moment, before he exploded. "Are you insane? I would never sign a law that enforces gun ownership!"

Charlotte looked at him for a moment, then opened the dossier dramatically, and began to read it out like a rap sheet. "Anti-gun, anti-abortion, anti-trans, anti-women, anti-gay… You're opposed to a lot of things. I'm willing to bet you're more anti-gay than anti-gun." And with that, she pulled Michelle towards her, and kissed her hard on the mouth, making sure the Senator saw every moment of it in detail. They spent five minutes lashing each other's tonsils with their tongues, before Charlotte pulled away and turned to the Senator again. "We can keep going at this. We'll only stop when you promise to vote for the President's gun legislation."

The Senator paled, and tried to look away, but couldn't as Charlotte had strapped his head in place. "No!" he said. "No, I'll be damned before I vote for that bill!"

Charlotte began kissing Michelle again, and unbuttoned her blouse, revealing her immaculate breasts beneath. The Senator squirmed uncomfortably, as Charlotte licked Michelle's nipples, and slipped her hand below the waistband of her shirt, fishing around for her moistening slit.

Michelle returned the sentiment, and soon both women were completely topless, and kissing deeply while touching each other's bodies sensuously. After a few moments, Charlotte once again addressed the Senator. "Are you ready to vote 'yes'?" she asked.

The Senator didn't reply.

Charlotte took this nonresponse as a no, and tore off Michelle's skirt completely, exposing her naked vagina to the Senator. She got down on her knees, kneeling before Michelle's womanly house of treasures. She made direct eye contact with Senator Danube, and stared him down as she poked her tongue out, and licked Michelle all the way from slit to clit, tasting her vaginal moisture.

Michelle groaned and gasped for added effect, and as the minutes passed by, she widened her legs, allowing Charlotte complete, unadulterated access to her most erogenous zones. Feeling her orgasm welling, she pulled Charlotte to her feet, and unzipped her black, skin tight pants, allowing her muff to be exposed, ready for her hungry mouth to devour.

Both Michelle and Charlotte maintained eye contact with the terrified-looking Senator this time. Charlotte was the first to speak. "Are you ready to vote 'yes', yet?" she asked, pausing to moan as Michelle continued smacking her lips on her clitoris.

The Senator began to cry, fat tears rolled down his wrinkled, craven face. But still, he did not answer the question.

Michelle stood up, and walking to her designer handbag, pulled out her trusty strap-on dildo. She maintained perfect eye contact with the frightened Senator, and walking around, monster prick waving about in front of her, she pulled over a chair. The chair was placed to the back was parallel to the Senators' direct line on sight.

Taking her cue, Charlotte bent over the back of the chare, exposing her labial plumpness to Michelle, inviting her strap-on inside her body. Michelle obliged. She began with the tip, before turning to the Senator and saying "I hope you're not ready to say yes – I'm very aroused for this, and I'd hate for you to interrupt our lesbian fuck fest."

The Senator continued to cry, and said plainly, "Oh Lord, why hast thou forsaken me with thine Horny Devils?"

Michelle plunged her fake cock deep into Charlotte, who gasped in response. She continued fucking her hard, the buckling rattling and jingling with every thrust. Charlotte's breasts kept jiggling violently, directly in the Senator's line of sight, making a loud slap each time they struck each other. Michelle kept fucking harder, and harder, pummelling into Charlotte until she moaned and screamed with ecstasy.

Just as Charlotte was about to climax, the Senator cried out "STOP!"

Michelle and Charlotte stopped immediately, and turned back to the Senator. Red Danube continued, "I'll vote for the bill, I'll do whatever you want! Just stop this abomination I see before me!"

Michelle uncoupled herself from Charlotte, and after wiping down the strap-on dildo and placing it back in her handbag, began to dress himself. The Senator, still crying was praying silently. When redressed, Charlotte turned to Red Danube and said "We're leaving. If I hear you breathe a word of what just happened here, I'll tell everyone you were involved." And with that they left the room, with the Senator still tied to the chair, and made their way back to their room to continue their fucking.

CHAPTER 11 – Truly Fucked

Day: Wednesday
Time: 1000 (local time)
Location: Seattle, WA

It was the day of the vote, when the Congress would pass the President's gun reforms, at approximately 3pm. Michelle and Charlotte were gathering themselves together in their hotel room in Seattle, readying themselves for a flight to Washington, where they would be congratulated by the President for a job well done. But then, just after 10am, Michelle's phone started ringing, with 'Unknown caller' displayed on the screen. Michelle answered without hesitation. "Hello, Michelle Morgan, Expert Negotiator."

"Michelle Morgan?" replied the voice. It was soft and raspy, as though it belonged to someone who had just smoked a packet of cigarettes, or a cigar, or even a joint. "Hello Michelle. I'm Becca Campbell. I believe you may have impersonated me at my own father's funeral."

Michelle's blood ran cold. How could she have found her number? What did this mean?

"Michelle," Becca continued, "I'm in the Washington office. I need you to come and meet with me, before this vote goes ahead, or I'll contact those Congress-people and force them to vote against the bill. You know where to find me." The phone hung up.

"We've got a problem," Michelle said to Charlotte, before reiterating what the caller had just told her. After some discussion, they decided it was best to go directly to Washington and confront Becca Campbell in person.

After a few short hours, their plane touched down, and Michelle and Charlotte were on their way to the Campbell Corp office in downtown Washington. "We need to do whatever, or whoever it takes to get this job done," said Michelle. "We'll have to come at this from every angle. We only have an hour until the Congress vote on the bill, and I won't let anybody get in the way of that!"

Charlotte nodded in agreement, then opened the door of the taxi, as they had arrived at the office. The two of them walked up to the reception desk, and Charlotte said, loudly, "We have a meeting with Becca Campbell. She's expecting us."

The receptionist directed them to the lift that would take them directly to Ms Campbell's new office, the one she had inherited from her father. The doors opened, and they stepped directly into Becca's office.

"Well, I'll admit I didn't expect you both to be here in time," she said, matter-of-factly. "Let's get down to business. I had to leave rehab early and unrehabilitated because you two have fucked things up for me. Speaking of, how did you know I was in rehab for, amongst other things, a sex addiction?"

Michelle responded. "I did what all good negotiators do – I went with my gut feeling."

Becca looked impressed. "And now, I am unrehabilitated, still battling my sex addiction, and you two beautiful women are in my office." She closed her eyes for a moment and breathed in and out deeply. "Now kiss," she said, looking directly at them.

Charlotte pulled Michelle towards her and kissed her hard on the lips. "Whatever, or whoever it takes, right?" she whispered so only Michelle could hear. They continued to kiss, and before long, they had taken each other's jackets off. Michelle could feel her pussy growing wet in her skirt, waiting to gush forth. Becca had definitely noticed, and she was ready to take it to the next level.

Becca came close to the women, and began kissing Michelle on her neck, before unbuttoning her blouse, exposing Michelle's stunning breasts and nipples. She continued kissing all the way down Michelle's midline, until she reached the thin layer of fabric that separated her mouth from Michelle's underlips. Unable to restrain herself, Becca ripped at the skirt, tearing it in twain, and set herself to town on Michelle's cunt.

Michelle and Charlotte continued kissing, and Michelle began to unbutton Charlotte's shirt, not wanting to miss out on any of the action. Becca rose, and started kissing Charlotte on the mouth, letting her taste Michelle's pussy on her tongue. This clearly worked for Charlotte, who's brassiere could no longer hold back her aroused breasts, as they burst through the clasp. Michelle began licking Charlotte's nipples, and with her hand reached into her pants and began to masturbate her vagina with her fingertips. After only a few moments, overcome with lust and desire, she fell to her knees and licked at Charlotte's slit as though it were the last time they'd ever see each other.

Charlotte began to disrobe Becca, and was surprised to see she had an excellent physique, with large, deep brown nipples, like dark fried eggs on her breasts. She worked on her left nipple with her tongue, rotating around it in circles. Taking her opportunity, Michelle lifted the front of Becca's miniskirt, and tearing her panties from her body, observed her pussy up close. She had a thick thatch of pubic hair, but Michelle didn't mind. She licked at her labia lovingly.

Becca groaned with the ecstasy of getting her clit and her nipples services at the same time.

Before long, all three women were completely naked, kissing each other and stroking each other's cunts. Becca lay down on her back on the desk, legs in the air, displaying her pussy like a peacock. Charlotte's fingers slipped inside her, and she fingered her, tapping aggressively on her G-spot. Michelle moved around the desk, and straddling Becca's face, pushed her labia to her mouth.

The desk creaked and groaned under the pressure, and rocked about so violently, it was almost certain to fall apart. The three women were groaning and shuddering, and moaning with pleasure. Charlotte indicated for Michelle to lay on the desk too, before putting her other hand to Michelle's dripping pussy and fingering her. Not missing her cue, Becca slipped her fingers into Charlotte's vagina, masturbating her. The room was filled with the scents of snatch and sex, as the women fingered and fucked each other, licking and slurping until each in turn orgasmed with a full-body shudder and moans that would have made a convent of nuns pray for the Armageddon to arrive and end their miserable existence. They recovered, gasping for air, heads swimming in the afterglow of their violent orgasmic explosions.

Michelle looked over to the clock on the wall. It was right on 3pm. The vote was happening right now! They had been fucking for so long, Becca hadn't had the chance to contact her Congress-people. Feeling even more satisfied now, Michelle gave Charlotte a high-five, and proceeded to wipe herself down of sweat and female fluids. Charlotte looked to the clock, and realised too what this meant. The only person who hadn't realised was Becca, who was busying herself with a bag of white powder. Michelle suspected she would be in rehab again before long. They left quickly before Becca noticed, and began to make their way to the White House.

The drive took over fifteen minutes, but once at the White House, Michelle and Charlotte were ushered through to the President's Oval Office with quick haste. The President's body guards lead them up the wide corridors to the office, where Michelle was hoping the President had received good news. By the time they got there, the vote had already happened. The President, Mr Geoffrey Nash, was on the phone, receiving the news of the vote. Michelle couldn't read his face at first, but then, a smile, a beaming smile. They had done it.

"Well done girls!" said the President. "It passed by two votes. I don't know how you did it, but I'm grateful for it! I'm going to arrange lifetime achievement awards for both of you; you've earned it. I can do that, you know. I'm very wealthy and I can make anything happen. The American people, true patriots with guns, thank and salute you for your efforts."

Michelle and Charlotte were so relieved it all went to plan. They had managed to pull off the biggest gun reform in American history in the space of a few days. But now they were exhausted and spent, and in desperate need of a rest.

The President continued, "it will take time for this new legislation to come into effect, but within the next few months, I expect to see every man, woman, and child, every teacher, every nurse, every god damn firefighter, carrying a gun so perfect, God himself may have crafted it! But for protection, of course. Protection from our enemies to the south…" The President continued to ramble for several minutes about the good work Michelle and Charlotte had done for the American people.

The moment was shattered when Michelle's phone began buzzing in her breast pocket. She looked, and saw it was Australia's Foreign Minister, Christopher Wayne calling. "I'll have to get this, I'm sorry," she said, before stepping outside the office, if only momentarily.

When she answered, the voice came down the phone quick and hurried, as though excited, or panicked, or both. "Michelle, it's Christopher Wayne here. Look, there's been some business here in the last few days and, I need your help and your expert negotiation skills, as soon as possible. Michelle, I'm challenging the Prime Minister for leadership of the Party. I'm calling for a leadership spill."

If you enjoyed Congressional Proclivities (The Gender-Flipped Version), please consider leaving a review on Amazon or Goodreads. What may take you a minute or so means far, far more than that for independent authors such as myself.

I do hope to see you again in the next Parliamentary Desires (The Gender-Flipped Version) book, Spilled Infatuations.

Until we meet again,

SPILLED INFATUATIONS

The Gender-Flipped Version
Parliamentary Desires Book 3

Amid leadership tensions and political rumblings in Canberra, specialist negotiator Michelle Morgan has been called back from the United States to assist Foreign Affairs Minister, Christopher Wayne, in a very important mission.

With an election looming, and the polling dismal, Minister Wayne has no option left but to pull the ultimate political power move, and challenge the Prime Minister for the leadership.

In her most demanding mission yet, Michelle will need to work her pussy to the bone to secure the Party ballot for Christopher Wayne, and receive her well-deserved reward.

It's a challenge that will take everything Michelle has to offer, and more. Follow Michelle, as she toys with men and woman of all persuasions, working hard to get Christopher Wayne in top position.

Can she tame the love rat Thomas Tucker? Will she neutralise Nadine Morris' unfulfilled desires? Find out, in Spilled Infatuations (The Gender-Flipped Version)!